CROOKED CREEK

Maximilian Werner

Torrey House Press, LLC
Utah

First Torrey House Press Edition, July 2011
Copyright © 2011 by Maximilian Werner

Published by Torrey House Press, LLC
P.O. Box 750196
Torrey, Utah 84775 U.S.A.
http://torreyhouse.com

International Standard Book Number: 978-1-937226-00-8
Library of Congress Control Number: 2011929745

Cover photos by Gul Tal, Guy Tal Photography, www.guytal.com
Back cover photo by Kim Werner
Cover design by Jeff Fuller, Crescent Moon Communications

For my mother and father

Not to have known — as most men have not — either
the mountain or the desert is not to have known one's self.
Not to have known one's self is to have known no one.

— Joseph Wood Krutch

CROOKED CREEK

PART ONE

After the rain had quit, the boy left the aspens, under which he sat with a shotgun and a nearly headless rabbit, and he strode through a field of alfalfa that wet him to his belt. Slung with a length of twine, the rabbit swung side to side over his shoulder. In the cool air, barn swallows gave way to bats as the dark bloomed. All about him the grass was pocked with horse droppings, and a coyote's howls drifted across the weeds and through the air to where the boy laid out the rabbit, and with his eyes and feet he hunted for wood in the outlying darkness.

On the edge of the field white box-hives stood together in the grass like the burial markers of many generations. In the wind's interims the drone of sleepy bees came to the boy's ears and to the ears of a dog that looked like it had been living hard. Drawn by the hot and salty smell of blood, it sat rigidly in the flickering light of the boy's fire. The boy then drew from a sheath on his hip a knife that threw firelight into the leaves of a branch overhead. He took up the rabbit by its hind legs and in the cool night he could feel the last hints of the rabbit's warmth on his wrist. He laid the rabbit in his lap like an unctuous scarf and it made a small pool by the toe of his boot.

As the dog looked on, the boy piled a load of damp wood on the fire, and then he sank the knife just below the rabbit's skin and ran its length. The knife pierced the rabbit's lung and from it a sough of air rose like an anti-soul into the smoke of the fire. The boy then tore out the organs and flung them to the dog. Earlier the boy had walked through an orb weaver's web and now its silk glistened on his face and his clothes steamed. He sat looking like some strange suborder of this world as the dog lay before him in the grass, filling his slender belly and growling even though the two-legged animal at the fire gave no sign that he would have it otherwise. In a low voice, the boy told the dog as much, and he pulled the rabbit from its damp integument. In the full glare of the fire, its pink and densely muscled body resembled a humanoid that had come into the world all wrong.

After the boy fed on the rabbit, he left the fire and the dog and trod toward the river to drink and wash. The sky had cleared and the moon's high and lowlands shone with equal brilliance, and its light ran on the water and on the painted backs of three Appaloosa horses that stood many hands high in the grass across the river. The boy drank long and deep. He could taste the silt and stones over which the river flowed. The piquant smell of wild mint, clover, and drying hay steeped the brume that lay upon the water, and in each mouthful he could taste some of that, too. Even in that dark he could see a brightly banded caterpillar drifting down river like nothing else in this world. After it had passed, the boy turned his eyes upriver as if waiting on another, and there, in a pool that whirled against the bank, the head of a drowned colt turned. He said "shit," spat, and wiped his mouth with the rough back of his hand. Then he climbed the stony bank and walked back toward the glow of the fire.

The dog had not moved. He lay in the wet grass panting and watching the boy poke and grow the fire into an ample light. The crickets made little of the night. He pulled up the collar of his slicker and bedded down beside the fire to wait on the arrival of his brother. Across the moon, a band of frayed and discolored clouds. The land still except for the long grass along the tree line that parted as if through it something were walking. But no eyes to happen on that place would find any reason to believe it.

Gil slept and dreamed. Above him both the moon and the sun. Crows cawed in the trees like macabre fruit. Then in a flurry of black snow, the crows quit their roosts and drifted overhead. Gil walked into a stand of ancient pines whose canopy was impaled with shafts of light, and in the dimness his eyes fell on a figurine interred to its waist in the loam. As he pulled the doll from the ground to better study it, the Earth made a small sigh in which he could smell something old and not to be bothered. The doll was carved of wood and wore a top hat and its face was soft, white, and sunken as if nothing were beneath it. When Gil looked on this visage he screamed, and as if wise to his horror, the doll awakened, its eyes widened, and it opened its mouth and mocked him until it seemed the doll alone were the screamer.

High on the mountains crowns of aspen burned in the dawn. As if autumn's currency or messages sent to the still-green world below, red and yellow and orange leaves rode down the dark and sleeping river. In the sky a ghost moon and a few pale stars and spiderlings drifting by on their web balloons. Where Cider stood he could see a group of does drinking up river, and though they were entrusted to the fog, the deer did not drink long, and one by one they returned to their covert of riparian growth. He reckoned they would stop and browse once hidden, but they did not. He listened to them go until they were gone and then made his way to where the river widened and was shallow enough for him to cross. There, on the beaten ground, fresh cow pies like smoldering fires, and the river still turbid where cattle had walked.

Though three years Gil's younger, Cider stood higher and was made of a heavier timber than his brother. The sun had done to his face what strong wind does to water. He made short work of the river even with his load. In the mud his tracks together with the tracks of many mammals and birds interlaced like vestiges of a saved world or afterlife where there was no fear and no blood to be lost. A few steers lingered and watched Cider cut up river along the arterial path that led to his brother. Then the steers turned and lowed at the sun rising over the mountains.

Gil's hair and the grass in which he slept were covered with hoarfrost. Judging by the color of the matter beneath the nails of one hand fallen out from under the blanket, Cider rightly reckoned his brother had not gone hungry. He shed his pack and with a stick stirred the ashes of the fire to articulate any coals that still burned there. Finding none, he pulled a folded sheet of coarse paper from his pocket and he tore it into strips and piled them together with small sticks in the ashes. Cider then took a saw and a length of twine from his pack and moved off through the field toward a ribbon of trees the ranchers had left alone for the sake of shade and demarcation.

There everything slept in rehearsal for the coming snows, and in the stillness Cider could hear leaves falling and hitting the forest floor. Fallen about him were young trees a beaver had felled, and from the breaches in many of their slender trunks the sap still flowed. He parted and bundled a tree that had been dead awhile and stuffed his pockets with wood chips fallen around the tree's stump. Through a clearing Cider saw that Gil had awakened. He shouldered the bundle of wood and made his way back to his brother's camp. Before he was well within hearing, Cider called out and Gil raised a closed hand and then opened it as if to say he had caught his brother's greeting and was now returning it.

The brothers spoke little as they prepared the fire and the morning meal. Cider spread the wood chips he had gathered over the coals, and upon the chips he set a cast iron pan. While the pan heated, the brothers ate goose jerky and got warm sitting between the fire and the sun. Gil rolled a cigarette and laid it on the toe of his boot to dry.

"What all you brought to eat?" he asked. Cider winked at him and with one hand he gave Gil his own last two cuts of jerky and with the other he pulled a cutthroat wrapped in paper from his pack.

"This is what all," Cider said. He held the trout out with both hands and with his thumbs he brushed away a few leaves and blades of grass that hid the fish's stippled markings. Cider told his brother where to find the bread as he gutted the trout. Deboned, the fish sizzled in the pan and turned from orange to pink like a splayed and smoking flower. The boys lifted the sweet flesh from its skin and put it in their mouths. Gil moved the pan to a cooling-stone between him and his brother and they finished off the trout and sopped their bread with the trout fat.

"You see a dog when you come up this morning, skinny looking mutt, yea big?" Gil asked, lighting his cigarette with one hand, showing size with the other.

"Nope," Cider said. "Thought about having Dime and Slowdee kick along with me, though. Thought 'nah, dogs wouldn't be worth waking Rance.' You think he wake and he wake, seems like."

"You done right Cide," Gil said, nodding.

"I was surprised he wasn't up before me, the way he been hunting you lately. I'll tell you what, he's either roostered up on hell's blood or he's crazy mean or both. Won't sit with Mama. Won't talk to her. Shit, Gil, I know the man's sour as pipe-rot, but what in hell'd you do to get him seeing red?"

Gil took a long drag of his smoke and looked out across the field.

"That dog sat up with me last night. He didn't fuss, didn't do nothing but lie right over there the whole night. Shared a rabbit with him. Wonder where he's gone to. Fire's hungry. Toss on some of that wood," Gil said.

"Snows will be coming, Gil. How long you expecting to stay out here?"

"I figured I'd go hole up at the autumn house when the weather make me. Place's still got the one good room there in back. Got a roof. Between you and the river, I'll eat alright. What'd you catch that cut on, anyway?"

"Deputy. You want a couple?" Cider dragged his hands through the wet grass and dried them on his pants. He then rose and walked the few feet to the pack. Returning to the fire, he opened the pack wide and from it he took a box of shotgun shells, four cans of beans, a tin of hashed beef, and a tightly rolled blanket. And from his coat pocket he produced the two flies, which he placed into Gil's hand.

"The beans and such oughta get you through until you can scare up some fish or something. I saw a clutch-a turkey when I come through here the other day. They fast," Cider said, shaking his head, "real fast."

"Yeah, they fast. But those fat bastards cain't outrun no shot," Gil said, studying the flies. "Real trouble is that they're smart. They know you're hunting them even before you actually hunting them. So there's that. Can't have no thoughts about them whatsoever until you're looking at one in your sights," he said, pointing a shotgun made of air.

"Remember when we couldn't walk through here without seeing a clutch or hearing a tom?"

"I surely do," Gil said. "Those were some damn fine hunting days, weren't they?"

"Yeah," Cider said, sort of troubled. "I wonder where they've gone to." He looked up toward the foothills as if the missing birds might be there.

"Someplace where they have cover, I reckon. Pop, Mama, and Jasper said that most of this valley used to be wooded." Gil swept the area with his hand.

"Well it's a shame that it's gone," Cider said.

"I'd say so." Gil pinched a bit of tobacco from his tongue.

"Well, I got to get on. I'll see you out at the autumn house in a few days, let whatever this is settle down a bit," Cider said, rising from the fireside and stretching his long arms into the sky.

"Appreciate you coming out, Cide. You get the mind to go moon-fishing, you let me know."

"Alright, then. A few nights from now we'll go. Me and them fish will give you an education," Cider said, raising his eyebrows.

"You know I need it. But we'll see who teaches who,

especially if the moon's got anything to say about it. River's different at night. What you know of it in the day ain't no count."

"Yeah, well, moon ain't never said much to me. I'll take your word for it though."

"Wish you wouldn't. Except for these things here, words are all I got left," Gil said.

Cider looked as if he could not decide on what to say and he shook his head three small shakes as he grabbed and slung the pack over his shoulder. Gil pressed his cigarette into the earth and put what remained in his shirt pocket.

"You don't need to say anything, Cide."

Cider toed the dirt.

"Yeah, well, I got to get on," he said.

"Alright then."

Cider took the path his brother had made through the field the night before. Gil did not watch his brother go. He gathered up his things and rolled stones and stood over the fire, and he doused the last flames with a deep yellow rope of piss. Columns of stinking and ice-colored smoke billowed about him, and like some novice magician's failed act of teleportation, when the smoke had cleared Cider was all but two strides from disappearing into the trees.

———✺———

Spent from the sun, Gil climbed down from the apple tree with his bag of fruit and he leaned it and his back against the dark and worn hip of the tree's trunk. Over the whine of pomace flies swarming some rotting fruit, Gil could hear Cider humming and his ladder knocking in the branches of a tree farther down the orchard. Fainter still he heard Rance's work-a-day curses. Dime and Slowdee were sprawled atop a mound of dirt on the edge of the orchard; so intent were they on watching some hidden thing across the field they did not rise when Gil forgot himself and called to them.

If all that were sour in the world had a voice it was Rance's. Each time that voice made the sound of his name, Gil felt sickened and certain that somehow he was being killed by it. Gil rolled his head around the tree and looked down the orchard and he saw Rance's pale face framed by the leaves like a baleful lantern.

"Why you sitting there like these apples 'ready been picked?" When Gil did not respond to his chiding, Rance cussed, and as he climbed down the ladder several apples dropped from his bag and made small thuds on the earth below. "Damnit boy, I'm gonna knock you on your brain-pan for making me come down there." Gil felt weakened by the sun and the heavy smell of apples, and though he knew he should, he could not rise.

Cider watched Rance empty his apples into a crate before walking toward Gil. He figured this meant he wasn't that angry, and he tested his theory by calling to him.

"You seeing any rusty apples on your end?"

Obscured by the leaves, only Rance's legs could be seen.

"Well hell no, an' you better not seen none neither. Trees've been sulfured three times in three months. Damn. Don't tell me you got rust up there." Rance took off his hat and beat it against his thigh. He walked beneath the tree to where he could see Cider.

"Well, I don't know. Take a look at this one here." Cider leaned from the ladder and dropped the fruit into Rance's hand. Rance mumbled and studied the apple.

"Ah shit, boy, this ain't rust. Wipes right off. It's pollen."

Rance looked up at Cider for an explanation.

"Like I said, I didn't know. If it was rust, figured you'd want to know about it," Cider said.

Rance shook his head and smiled meanly.

"Boy, your pa didn't learn you too well did he? If you can't tell the difference between rust and pollen, maybe you'd better just stick to loading. But I reckon you'd fuck that up too." Rance took half the apple in his mouth and chucked what remained at Cider. The apple struck his calf and left a moon-shaped stain on his pant leg.

"God damn." Cider was more surprised than injured, which he feigned by rubbing his calf.

"God ain't got nothing to do with it. He stays clear of this orchard. Like I told Him to."

After Rance turned his back, Cider looked at Gil, and when he saw that Gil saw him he winked and made a contorted grimace. Gil swallowed his laugh and looked up at Rance, who was now looking at him as if he were a waste.

"Look at you. You look like a heap of dead weeds. Git yer ass on up to the house and get us something to eat."

Gil pulled himself up using the tree and he slogged toward the house. Once he had cleared the orchard the dogs rose from their piling and followed him at a distance and he could hear them panting and Rance hollering, "And check on your ma."

Inside the house was cool and dark save where midday light shone through curtained, south facing windows. It smelled of mustard plaster, molded wood, night sweats and drying fever herbs, dust, dirty dishes, and a week-old bouquet of elephant heads, bog-orchids and yellow monkey flowers that Cider had gathered for his bedridden mother. Gil walked lightly to the icebox and from it he took a pail of water. As he drank, silver threads fell from his mouth's corners. He could feel the liquid loosen his tongue and wash over his insides and down his neck like a penetrant rain. Having drunk too fast, he was about to give it all back when he heard a muffled cry from his mother's end of the house. He listened for anything forthcoming. Then he swallowed hard to keep the rain in him, and he poured what remained into a cup and walked to his mother's room.

Gil stood outside her door and listened to her breathe as if she were submerged in mud. When he opened the door, he saw she had slipped halfway from the bed. Her gown was bunched to her waist and her stomach was gibbous with sunlight. He had been watching it rise and fall for what seemed like a long time when a bark came in through an open window and startled him back into the room. He placed the cup of water on the bed stand and saw that her stomach shined with a dew-like sweat. After he looked into her face and saw that it slept, he ran his hand over her stomach as if to dejewel it. He then wrapped his hands around her nearly deer sized ankles and lifted her legs back onto the bed.

As he pulled down her gown, he spoke to her in a whisper. "Brought you something cool to drink, Mama, right here," he said. "You ain't got no business trying to get up. Me and Cider will tend to you until you're well again." He looked her over. "Your gown come up, Mama. Don't worry, I'll cover you. You thirsty?" But she lay there as if between two worlds and did not stir as Gil covered her.

Over places where sweat lay, her nightgown sank and darkened until her body looked lunar beneath it. Gil studied each dark patch. The contagion had left no visible mark on her body, still brown and firm and soft as packed dust. Outside a bank of clouds blotted out the sun and when the room darkened

Gil rose from his mother's bed and walked to the window. In the air the smell of dust and rain and rain-laden sage. Hair thin needles of lightning striking hills to the south. Gil closed the window and latched it and returned to his mother's side.

Her eyes had opened. When he moved over her to see if those eyes saw, he smelled the odor of shit. "Damn, Mama, you messed yourself," he whispered. He went to the kitchen to get some water and rags, and Sara lay there like a soiled and goose-fleshed effigy of the damned.

Gil drowned the pail in an open cask his father Preston had built the year of his death, and he took rags made from a pair of his father's trousers and he walked back to his mother's room. He lit a candle and its light faltered as if it were not sure that it should be there. Once the flame steadied, he placed the pail of water on the foot of the bed. Again he spoke to her in a whisper and he told her what he was going to do and not to be afraid and he slipped the straps of her gown over her shoulders and worked it off like a slough.

Gil dampened a rag and rolled his mother on her stomach. A dark rill had formed beneath her. He wiped it as best he could from the sheets, and even in the dimness he could see small gold hairs that shined like marigold pollen on the small of her back. As a girl, Sara was kicked by a horse, and except for the silver, moon-shaped scar below her heart, her skin was smooth and unbroken. And yet the soles of her feet and hands looked like they had lived much longer than forty years, and when Gil poured the water like some nostrum between her legs her toes curled and her hands seized the sheets and did not let go until the pouring ceased.

He tore a large rag in half and with it he wiped away feces and water that had gathered in the creases of her buttocks, and as he did so his mother made his name. When he asked if she were awake she did not respond. If that sound meant he was doing wrong he could not tell, and he paid it no mind as he turned her on her back and lifted her leg up by her ankle and rested it on his shoulder where her pale and supple calf hung as though it were filled with milk. The skin of her inner thigh reddened where he had run the rag across it, and thinking the cloth too coarse, he wet a corner of the sheet and set to cleaning the rest of her.

So absorbed was he in the sound of his own and his mother's breathing he did not hear Rance enter the house nor open his mother's door. Rance was on him now. He took Gil by the hair and yanked him off the bed. He would not let go. He kicked him in the face and stomach and shouted some maniacal obloquy, and Gil knew the man was finally going to kill him. He looked up long enough to see how Rance stood and when he saw that Rance faced him he punched him squarely in the groin. Rance made an animal sound and dropped to his knees, and he held himself with one hand and Gil's hair with the other. Gil spun around and planted his hands on the floor behind him and he put his boot to Rance's head. When Rance reeled back from the blow, Gil broke free and dove like a crazed and bloodied bird through the window-glass.

Cider sat whittling beneath a tree on the edge of the orchard. He heard the glass breaking and saw his brother pick himself up from the ground and move at a broken run across the field. The dogs saw him too. They did not recognize his gait and the hair on their shoulders rose and they bolted toward him through the knee high grass. Cider called to them and Gil cast a sidelong glance and saw the dogs coming for him. He yelled their names lest they keep mistaking and tear him asunder.

The dogs began to trot but they were still growling. Seeing this, Gil slowed to a walk and called to them as calmly as he could. When they had come within twenty feet, they raised their heads to smell him out. Recognizing his scent, they turned and headed back toward Cider. Gil whispered "sweet Jesus" and moved off toward the river.

The dogs approached Cider proudly. He took them by the hispid scruffs of their necks and held them for fear they would bolt again.

"Where you heading?" Cider yelled.

Gil slowed and hollered back.

"One of two places...you know them both."

Cider's brow furrowed and he turned and walked the dogs toward the house. He looked at the window through which his brother had flown and there, framed by the broken glass, was Rance. He was breathing heavy, and blood from a cut above his eye curtained half his face. Then he slumped like some miscreant deity who had just made himself a world he was now too weak to live in.

<hr />

A horizon of pines stretched like a saw-blade in the gloaming. Beyond them, a meadow and a house sullied with bullet holes and fire and time. Gil moved toward it and on either side of him the wind fussed in the blue-black grass. Shaggy mice sat watching on their haunches in their autumn coats. A pair of finches broke from their bower and flittered overhead in the moribund light. Though the door was unlocked, it would not open, and Gil followed a well-worn path until he came to a fallen wall. He passed into the house and walked into a large room whose plaster walls were wavy and yellowed from soot and water.

Glass from the room's only window was gone, and in its corner was a web in which hung the twilight husks of many insects and small copper leaves and a young bird that by its colors seemed the offspring of the kind he had seen outside. The bird's bright wings were wrapped thickly to its sides, and like a knife-blade, its beak was folded into its breast feathers where it could do no harm. As Gil studied the gray art that enshrouded its head, one of the bird's dark eyes opened and looked at him. He took a step back and heard someone walking the floor of the room above him. He saw that he had no shoes and that his teeth were falling into places where he could not reach them.

The room in which he heard the walking was lit by a fire although there was none, and where the roof had once been there was now night sky that wheeled overhead. Gil looked about the room for some sign of the walker, and high on a charred ladder that leaned against the wall he saw his mother climbing. Her hair was white and frail as ash and her skin shined like sulfur-rich coal. When she neared the place where the ladder vanished against the night, she turned and looked down at Gil.

"Come with," she said.

He looked at the ladder and back at her.

"That ladder won't hold me, Mama."

———— ❦ ————

The full moon rose with the setting of the sun. It had been up for some time as Cider quietly packed his things, grabbed his rod, and climbed out his window by its light. Behind him he could hear the house settle in the cold. He walked to the far edge of the yard where the dogs were tethered to an old spring-tooth harrow that was bushy with long dead grass. As he neared them, the dogs let out a low whine from somewhere under the harrow and, trailing their ropes behind them, they crawled out with ears flat and tails between their legs. They each licked his hands as he reached to untie them.

Cider held Slowdee by the loose skin above his neck and he ran his hand over the top of his head to check it. The dog winced and broke from his grasp. He spoke softly to the dog and got him to come round again, and he got down on his knees and held the dog's head with both hands and turned it to the light. As he studied the welt above the dog's right eye, he said "damn." That Rance had beat him good. Cider whispered to Dime and the dog walked cautiously toward him. In the clear crisp light he saw that the dog's chest and jowls were still crusted with blood from the pig he'd killed hours before.

Rance had won a Duroc hog on a bet, and when she farrowed for the first time it was like she was dying. The dogs heard the ruckus and they broke from their pen and charged the farrow stall that Rance had thrown together with old boards and chicken wire. Bristling, the Duroc rose to meet them with a piglet hung halfway out her backside that made a small, dark grammar to the world and the get that lay below. While Slowdee barked at the sow, Dime snuck round and he broke through the slats of the stall and snatched a piglet that had already dropped and he crushed it and then began to devour it. The Duroc turned and looked at the dog finishing one of her young, and lest the dogs kill them all, she began to cannibalize her litter and had eaten two before Rance could come and do anything to stop her.

Cider let Dime loose and rose from the cold earth that wet his knees. He looked back at the house for some sign of

Rance waking. There was none. He turned and led the dogs toward the tree line to get them out of the moonlight. There he bucked off his pack and fished a stone from inside his boot. The dogs paced and whined a little ways off. Cider told them to hush as he urinated on a hoof-beaten patch of scrub oak. He then shouldered his pack and walked the seam that ran between wood and field toward the autumn house. Slowdee and Dime trotted around to the scrub oak and pissed where Cider had, and when they caught up with him, they slowed then bolted ahead. He called to them in a strong whisper, but they ignored him and soon they were gone from his sight.

The air was cold and sharp and the few clouds overhead drifted east. When he reached the head of the woodland path, Cider stopped and listened for the dogs. He heard the flutelike sounds of bog toads and heard stones rolling in the river that flowed farther off. He moved quickly through the dark band of pines and crossed a small field of cattle-cropped grass on whose far corner the autumn house was built. For the fourteen years Cider had been in the world the house had been abandoned, and except for the north wall where in daytime the sun did not show, it hosted vines that hid and weighted its rotted timbers. On the roof a mulch of leaves from as many autumns rustled, and where a branch had fallen there was a hole through which moonlight and leaves and weather fell.

When he got to within a few yards of the house, Cider stopped and called to Gil. When no answer came, he called to the dogs. He scanned the tree line. When he saw that they were not forthcoming, he climbed the front steps whose soft planks sagged beneath his weight. Mud nests hung like hives in the nooks above, and from them steel-blue swallows worried and darted as Cider lifted away the door and walked into the house. Again he called to Gil and heard nothing but the tick-ticking of mice and a small wind sounding through the house's many breaches and glassless windows. The house grew darker as Cider made his way to the back room. By what light ran thinly across the floor, he could not see, and he lit a candle and followed it into the room.

In the corner a pile of sticks and a fire pit filled with ash. Cider leaned his rod against the wall and eased the pack from his shoulders. He then held his hand just above the coals and felt no warmth. He walked with his candle to the other side of the room where Gil had spread his blanket. There he lit three candles that Gil had placed on the floor, and he squinted at their flames then looked away while his eyes adjusted to the light.

On the wall Cider saw distorted forms, strange figures, and pieces of words scribed in coal. He could not even guess at their meaning. Outside the moon was directly overhead and its light erased the stars and deepened the shadows of trees. Figuring Gil had gone to the river without him, Cider left the house and took the path that lead there.

He passed a woodshed on whose door hung a bovine skull and farther down what may have been a familial necropolis made with aspens that looked silver and swollen in the light. The path ran into a band of trees that stood between him and the river. In there he heard the muffled growls of dogs. Cider stopped at the top of a knoll down which the path descended, and below where that knoll ended was an ax-hewn clearing whose edge was lined with a rotted cord of wood. Against it he saw Gil's slumped and silent form and a dog Cider did not recognize stood over him and its hair was raised high and it growled at Dime and Slowdee as they circled around him.

Cider yelled at the dog that guarded his brother. It turned to him and its teeth flared in the light and he saw that its face was damp with blood. He continued to yell and clap his hands, but the dog would not scare. He picked up a stone and hurled it. When it struck the dog's backside, he whirled around to meet his attacker and then he backed over Gil's body and watched Cider and the other dogs. Cider searched the trees and he found a heavy pine branch, and with it he walked toward the dog, shouting and striking trees and bushes. Distracted by the noise, the dog did not see Dime and Slowdee coming, and when Cider was within a few yards, Slowdee nipped the dog's spine and together they drove him off.

Gil sat on the ground with his shotgun resting longwise and upward between his legs, and his head was savaged in the back and had fallen to one side. Where blood did not cover it, Gil's down-turned face was stone-gray, and it glowed with earthshine. Cider crouched down in front of him and he repeated the Maker's name. Gil's mouth was filled with congealed blood that flowed out like some strange libation for a defunct god, and it dried into an orb as if he wore a small dark apple around his neck.

The dogs had returned from chasing the stray and Cider looked at them and saw that their faces were also bloody. He screamed half-crazed curses and took the shotgun from his brother's lap and pulled the triggers. Both barrels of the gun were empty and Cider threw it at the dogs like an ax. The gun did not strike them, but they ran back into the trees and they did not approach him again. Cider returned to Gil and he asked him what he should do and he pleaded with the corpse as if he knew the language of the dead. Said there was little chance their mother would recover, but that it was still a chance, and whether his death would destroy it, Cider did not know, and could they wait on telling her until she grew stronger, and would that be alright, brother?

The moon was now low in the western sky and Cider took Gil by the wrists and pulled him up onto his shoulders. He carried him through the trees and across the river toward the plot of ground where his father's and uncle's bodies were buried, although the precise whereabouts of their graves had vanished. There Cider used his knife to hack away a grave and he worked the night to get it done by dawn. Cider tended to his brother's clothing and he spat on the cuff of his shirt sleeve and wiped the blood from his face that the river had not washed away. He eased Gil into the grave and when he was interred, Cider did not pack the earth. As if one day his brother would wake from this sleep.

※

Westerlies had turned late autumn rains into snow, and if not for the burrow holes of pot-guts and black weeds the snow could not cover, it would have seemed as though no autumn or other world had ever been. As if the snow offered Sara the warmer blanket, she rose from her bed late in the night and walked barefoot out into the yard and lay down beneath the stars. Rance found her the next morning just as the sun was rising, and where her body was not covered, her skin was frost-blue and her eyes were open and glassed with ice. He walked back to the house and jarred Cider from his sleep.

"Yer ma quit us in the night. Get up," Rance said.

"What in hell. . .Mama what?"

"Get yer boots on and meet me in the yard."

Cider did not weep as they worked. When Sara was freed from the earth, Rance insisted they carry her to the barn where her body would stay cold until they could get it buried. Cider looked back at the house and then at Rance. He bent down

and slipped his arms beneath his mother's knees. Rance raised
the latch and pushed the door open with his shoulder, and they
muddled through the dark toward a packing table at the rear
of the barn. They laid her down the table's length and Rance lit
a lantern that hung overhead. In its light she looked wall-eyed
and wore a strange grin. "Shut her eyes," Rance said, and he
walked out of the lantern's light.

Cider placed his hand on his mother's frozen eyes and
when the lids were warm he closed them and listened to Rance
fumbling and cussing in the dark. Cider looked at his mother
and she was still lovely in death. She was wearing a silver
necklace with a small key on it and he quickly unclasped it and
put it in his pocket. When Rance returned carrying an apple
crate, his face was red and shining with sweat. Cider looked at
the crate and wondered out loud if his mother would fit in it.
Rance stared at him as though he had asked if the moon would
fit in the sky. "Hell yes she'll fit in it. Now get up to the house
and get her some clothes." The dogs sat outside the barn door,
watching, and when Cider approached them on his way back
from the house they slunk off.

To his chest he held a linen dress and the deerskin shoes
his mother was wont to wear in summer. He walked into the
barn and placed them on the crate. Her body had begun to thaw
and from it wisps of steam rose and disappeared. Rance eyed
the clothing, perhaps remembering its origins, and gestured to
Cider to come to the body and together they got her dressed.
Sunlight fell on them now through the open door, and when
he saw that she would not fit, Rance said "Confound it" and
that he wasn't buying no coffin and he shoved Cider toward
her feet and told him to lift. They walked her over the mouth
of the crate and lowered her in. Lengthwise the crate was too
short and Rance rolled her on her side and bent her knees and

he lifted the crate's lid into place and held it there.

"There anything you want to say," Rance asked.

Cider watched his mother's face in the shallow light. He made a small prayer. But like some newfangled apparatus found in a dream, he could find no way to use it. Rance nailed the crate shut and from the barn wall he took down a pick-ax and shovel and leaned them on the crate. He looked at Cider.

"Going into town. Got to tell someone should anyone come wondering."

Cider stared at the crate.

"You got any sense at all you'll get started on that hole while the weather's with ya," Rance said, banging the mud from his boots. "Where is that brother of yours? Get him to help."

"I don't know," Cider lied, and he took up the tools and bore them on his shoulder. He walked out of the barn toward the nameless boneyard where his brother, father, and uncle lay.

"Where you going with them tools?" Rance barked.

"I'm going to our plot," Cider replied, "like Mama wanted."

Rance's face reddened.

"Not by my account," he said. "Where she bury is my decision and no one else's. She's going in the orchard clearing."

"That's shit and you know it," Cider said. He let the tools fall into the snow. "You can dig your own damn hole to hell or anyplace you see fit, but she ain't going in it."

"Damn you, boy." Rance rushed out to where Cider stood and he picked up the tools with one hand and took Cider by the arm with the other and he walked him hard across the yard to the end of the orchard. There Rance dropped the tools and pushed down Cider.

"Boy, if you've a mind to stay in the world you'll have that hole dug by morning."

———— ∞∞ ————

Piles of clouds had blown down from the north and settled in the basin, and by their and night's cover Cider snuck out to the barn. Inside he closed the door and lit a candle. He heard pigeons cooing in the rafters as he walked to the barn's far corner where old boards and fence posts were stacked. He spied two posts and slipped them from the pile and carried them to the packing table. From his pack he took a wool blanket and spread it out across the table in the candle's light. He took up the posts and laid them on either side of the blanket, into which he rolled them and then wrapped them with twine. Earlier that evening, Rance had returned from town drunk on hell's blood and he'd slogged off to bed. Still, Cider worked quickly because he knew that Rance was all foul darkness now.

A cold rain had begun to fall and it made a wooden music as it struck the roof and walls. Above him the pigeons were spooking and he told them to settle as he set to prying the lid from the apple crate. Cider tipped the crate and rolled his mother out on the barn floor. Her body was stiff and heavy. He straightened her as much as she would allow. Then he filled the crate with sacks of mulch-apples to take her place. When the crate felt like she was in it, he replaced the lid and he then carried his mother to the barn door and left her in the dust while he gathered his things and erased all signs that he had been there. His ear to the door, Cider heard only the rain. He put his head out and looked for anything his ears could not tell him. Nothing stirred except a barn cat whose belly dragged in the snow as he drifted across the yard.

Cider stood in the doorway with his mother over his shoulder and he held her there with one arm and the tools and stretcher beneath the other, and should Rance see drag marks when he finally awoke from his drunken slumber, Cider bore these things across the yard to where the field began. The waning moon wavered like an eye under water and beneath it Cider pulled his pale load across the field. At its edge, impresses left by bedding deer. He stopped to get his breath and figure the night's age, and he judged there was no time for standing there.

Tracks of the rogue dog crisscrossed Gil's grave, and at the grave's head the faint tailing of a hole the dog had been digging. Cider looked around to see if he was still about. He cleared away the snow from his mother's would be grave. The ground did not give beneath his feet, and so he dropped the shovel in the snow and took up the pick-ax and brought it down hard on the Earth. The pick stuttered and cleaved its width in dirt. He studied the chunk to see if it got softer but it did not, and he chucked it and circled to the head of his brother's grave. The dog's hole was a dark reminder in the snow. Cider sunk his bare hand down in it and the earth there felt crisp and grainy but it had not frozen. He looked at his mother and then at the moon, which had moved the space of twice its size. There would not be time.

He set to excavating his brother's grave and when it lay open he brushed the dirt from his brother's face. Gil looked calm and boyish, and while it made his death seem a benign thing, Cider looked away as if it were the face of a Judas corpse. He climbed from the grave and readied his mother's body and from the stretcher he took the wool blanket and wrapped her in it. Cider lashed its ends and then lowered her and the two posts into the hole. He looked down at the amalgam he had made and he spoke to the corpses. Told them why he'd done what he'd done and gave his word he'd do otherwise come spring. To the east the sky was paling. Cider refilled the hole and packed the grave with his feet. And he left no marker so that no one would find them out. So that nothing could take away their right to darkness.

PART TWO

When he awoke, the locomotive had carried him deep into the country and into the dark of that country's night like a horse its sleeping rider. He eased himself down and stood listening to the cattle moan and move heavily in their cars whose sides shined and stank with piss and shit that had sloshed through the floor vents. A few low camp fires burned untended, and beyond the pale tincture of their light fallen upon saguaro and agave and soil red as rust, it seemed the world had yielded to some ineffable void to which he now stood initiate. He looked down the tracks and saw that no one was about and with his belongings he walked to the front of the train and crossed the tracks toward a small depot made of new and finely ripped pine from the north.

A faint light fell from the building's front window and as he neared it he could smell the timbers and paint and the sun-soaked skins of rattlesnakes stretched and pinned across the door. He wiped the dust from the window and looked in. An oil lamp turned to low burned in the center of a table with four chairs, two of which were drawn. On the table what seemed to be a book or ledger. A door partly opened onto a room in the back and through it he saw a cot and upon it a skinny man whose bare legs showed from his knees down. The man did not move, but above him the shadow of some other presence sawed and wheeled and made strange repetitions until the man's feet knocked against each other and were still.

He stepped back from the window and glanced side to side as if to decide which way he would run should it come to that and he heard the muted sounds of talking and the knock of boots on floorboards. He turned back to the window and saw a man standing in the center of the room wearing a coarse apron and holding a dripping rag in his hands, looking at him. He walked backward and fell from the porch. More talking. Lamplight. Footsteps. As he picked himself up he saw the man's face against the pane of glass through which he had been looking. He ran into the desert. Jackrabbits broke from their hiding places. His breath leapt. He ran on. Past the silent camps of rail workers. Their laundry and dead fires. White canvas tents like ghost houses.

———— ∞ ————

To the south, lowland grass fires were blackening the country. The wind had worked them the night long and by morning it had driven smoke and ash some hundred miles north where it settled all about him. He stood and shook ash from his hair. A breeze rose from below the escarpment upon which he had stopped for the night, and in it he could smell the leafy sweetness of cottonwoods and moving water. With his blanket hanging from his shoulders he walked to where the ground fell away in small rivulets and the breeze strengthened.

The tracks he made in the ash were shy of antecedents, as if he had been born of some union between the ground and the night. He made a roof for his eyes with his hand and he watched a pair of hawks drift in overlapping circles against the smoke-blunted sun. Below locusts caught gusts of wind that blew them clacking wildly across the draw. He slid down the escarpment on his boot heel and walked through the blonde stalks of spent cattails toward the river.

The water was cold and clear and quiet. He shucked off his boots and propped his pack against the trunk of a Palo Verde, marveling at the smooth greenness of it. He had seen his share of trees in his life but none like this, and he half expected the river to bewilder him somehow as he waded out to his waist and sat. When the sandy floor of the river calmed he could see the shadows and the sudden flaring of fish. He leaned back and the river ran over him and into his mouth and he let it carry him a few yards and he then got to his feet and moved toward shore. Sunfish hunted minnows in a pocket of slow and shady water along the bank and when they spooked at his approach the water churned and their bodies glinted like sinking coins.

After the fish had cleared he saw what he thought was a stone, but since there were no others around, he bent until his eyes were just above the water. A lone sunfish hovered above the ruptured and opal dome of a child's skull. Whether it was the grave of some rover's or settler's child he did not know, but he figured natives of that place wouldn't bury where the body would likely get washed away. They would know better. He looked for some marker that bore the child's name but saw nothing. He sank his hand and waved it down the child's length to clear the sand, and as he did so he saw eye-holes fringed with silt and the cocoons of flies.

The child's coat and pants wagged and the tongues of its rawhide shoes waved in the current. The coat's pewter buttons had sunk into the soft bone of the child's sternum and its hands lay at its sides like strange fossils of crabs. Buttoned into one of the child's coat pockets was a small wooden trunk. He stood and looked up and down river. A heron glided in as if to land, but then saw him and squawked and rose back into the air and flew on. The sun had moved directly overhead and the river glared with its light. He looked down at the trunk.

When he got it to shore he saw that the trunk was not made of wood but of a dark epidermis. Like the skin of a life form harvested from the sea. He wiped it down with his shirt sleeve and held it up and turned it in the light. A symbol like those he had seen in the rail camps and the garbage heaps of Chinese workers was embossed on the trunk's lid. Seams beveled and sewn with coarse thread. Horn or bone fastenings. A seal of wax. He laid the trunk in the sand and unsheathed his knife. He looked around. On a branch above a blue belly lizard warmed itself in the sun. Its eyes closed. He took the knife and carefully ran its tip around the lid. The seal broken, he moved to his knees and unclasped the trunk's fastenings.

Inside was a box the size of a deck of cards and what seemed to him a hoary and exotic cloth doll. She wore a layered dress and her face was pretty and painted on and her skin was the color of straw. Her black hair had been braided into chains and sat coiled atop her head. He felt each layer of her dress and there were two in all. The first fine as muslin. The second and closest to her skin coarse as burlap. "What manner of thing. . ." Held upside down, the doll became another and it was not beautiful. Its face had no mouth nor finery and what were the red shoes of the first doll were now the red hands of the other. He laid her back in the trunk. The box was wrought from copper and glowed as if with oil from the child's hands. He depressed a nub of copper to unlock it and as he opened the box he saw a snake moving inside and he startled and dropped it into the sand.

The box lay open and he watched the snake and waited for it to glide out but it did not. He squatted and poked at the box with a small stick and when the snake did not stir he took the box back into his hands. The snake was a succession of silver vertebrae connected to hidden wires and pulleys. When the box was opened the machinery turned and the snake undulated in flesh-like mimicry. A dust devil rose and whirled and disappeared a few yards off shore. He closed the box and walked down to the river. In the shallows, shadows of leaves and dead and drinking dragonflies. Gnats and sunfish had come back to hang above the child's skull.

———— ❧ ————

The sun had not yet risen and the man they called JD went into Garvey's room to wake him. Garvey lay with his hands folded across his barrel chest. His clothes and boots were still on and his hat was tipped to his chin. JD lit an oil lamp and made it burn low and he said Garvey's name. When he did not wake, JD grabbed the toe of his boot and shook it.

"Garvey. Get up. We've been robbed. Come on now."

Garvey sat up and his hat fell to the floor. He looked straight at JD. His eyes red. Cotton-mouthed, his tongue clicked when he spoke.

"We ain't been nothing." He looked around. "You woke Seth yet?" Garvey asked.

JD had turned and was walking into the front room of the depot.

"No. He was in a bad way last night. I figured best just to wake you." JD walked over to the stove and looked down into a pot that sat there: "This coffee?"

"What all was took?" Garvey asked as he stood in the doorway and tucked in his shirt.

JD turned and faced him squarely.

"Damned if I know. Mules were actin' up. Went down there and seen the boarding we done stripped away. Couple crates were busted open there toward the front. There could have been more in back. But I didn't have no light and wasn't walking the shaft without one. That's when I come and got you."

Garvey looked down at his boots and he cocked them each in turn as if to admire them. He looked up at JD.

"You ain't told anyone else then, just me?"

"Just you."

The two stared at one another.

"Alright then." Garvey walked across the room and rapped on Seth's door with his knuckles.

"Seth, you awake?" The two men stood there, listening. "Seth?" Garvey looked at JD. "What'd you say he was drinking?"

"I guess a few jars were going around," JD said.

Garvey opened the door and looked in, but the room was empty.

Outside the air was cold and men from the company stood around their fires drinking coffee and staring early-eyed into the flames. Others still slept or coughed or dressed in their tents. Garvey and JD approached the first fire and Garvey asked the men there if they had seen Seth. Two of the younger men chuckled. No one spoke. Garvey spat and joined their circle. He put out his hands as if to hold down the flames and he looked from man to man.

"Which of you sonsabitches knows where Seth is?" he asked. The younger men looked down at their boots. Garvey looked straight at them and leaned toward them over the fire. "I ain't going to ask you again."

A new man Garvey did not know rose from where he had been crouching by the fire.

"Like me, these boys know more than what they done. The man you're looking for's over there, behind those rocks." He motioned with his chin. Garvey watched him. JD headed toward the rocks. The man whipped his coffee cup to empty the dregs and he looked at Garvey. "If you don't need nothing else I'd like to get some track down before the sun come up."

Garvey spat into the fire and wiped a thread of spittle from his chin. He asked the man for his name, but before he could get it JD called to him from the rocks.

"He's up here Garvey. Best bring a man with a shovel."

Garvey turned to one of younger men and told him to get up there with a shovel and the young man did as he was told. Garvey again looked at each man and he then walked into the failing darkness toward the rocks.

Seth lay buried to his chin. The wind had blown sand the night long and grit ringed his mouth and caked his eyebrows. A dozen empty bottles and jars were arranged around him and when the breeze picked up they made a sorry music. Piss holes riddled the mound. Garvey said "shit" and he motioned to the man with the shovel. "Clear him off."

When he had finished clearing away the dirt, the man stepped back and leaned on his shovel. The three of them looked down at Seth. Sunlight now fell faintly across the desert. Saguaro and sandstone knolls trailed long shadows. JD glanced at the sun and looked at Garvey.

"They'll be pulling the train out around noon. What do

you want to do?" JD asked.

Even as Garvey spoke to the boy with the shovel, he did not take his eyes off Seth.

"Get yer skinny ass back to camp."

"Yes sir."

When the young man had gone, Garvey turned to JD.

"I got an idea who busted in there."

"Yeah?"

"Yeah."

"Those boys?"

Garvey shook his head, no.

"A feller I saw last night. Peeking through the window. He must have come off the late train, and he might have seen me washing one of them wagon burners." Garvey took a block of tobacco from his vest pocket and bit off a piece and replaced it. "Who been making the late run? Tom?"

"Yep." JD crouched down beside Seth and gave his cheek a hard slap. "Damn he smells."

"When Tom come in tonight you tell him to stop over."

"Alright," JD said. "What do you want to do with this sack here?"

"Let's get him up."

Garvey bent down and took Seth up by the arm pit and he nodded to JD that he do the same and together they got him up and walked him through camp to the depot.

"He ain't going inside," Garvey said. They steered Seth toward the depot steps and once there they turned and sat him down.

"I'll get him some fresh clothes. You go round back and get me a bucket of water," Garvey said.

"You want to go down and see what all was taken? That train will be here directly."

"Hell yes I wanna. But Seth the only one who could say what was took. He packed them crates. . . . Shit. Don't remind me about no train."

JD looked to the west where the men were working. A chain of them were passing sections of track and singing.

"You hear me? That conductor don't need to know nothing about why or what he waiting on. Just give him a couple a greenbacks and tell him to settle." Garvey dug some folded bills from his pants and counted out three and he stuffed them in JD's shirt pocket. "Here. If there is any worrying to be done, you let me do it. Now get going."

After Garvey and JD had gone, a blonde mongrel dog crawled from under the depot steps, yawned, and looked around. Seth had come to and he and the dog stared at one another. The dog sniffed the air. Its skin alternately shined and darkened where it fell over and between its ribs. Trickles of blood had dried and flaked on the inside of its rear leg. "By the looks of you, I'd say we were at the same party last night." The dog ears twitched and he circled around to the steps and stopped at Seth's feet.

Seth watched him. The dog then sniffed Seth's boot. "What in hell are you up to. . .?" Seth sat up and saw the dog licking something from his boot. He tried to pull away and the dog growled. Seth leaned his head back on the steps. The dog resumed licking and growling as he did so. A bank of black nimbus clouds were dropping rain and drifting in from the southwest. Seth closed his eyes. "God if I ain't been damned to hell."

⚬⚬⚬

After a meal of beans and jerked beef, he took his tin to the river and scrubbed it with sand. The air smelled of smoke and river mud. Lizards raced through the hot dead grass and their whip-like tails left furrows in the sand. He had washed his clothes and hung them in a mesquite tree to dry and when the wind gusted they flapped and twisted in the branches. He put the tin in his pack and walked to his clothes. As he pulled them on something came crashing through the brush. He dove toward his pack and drew his knife. Then he lowered it. A large black goat stood on the bank above and stared at him. It had been hobbled and wore a tin bell. He listened and when he determined the goat was alone he spoke to it. "You're likely to get yourself killed barging in on someone like that."

The goat took a few labored steps down the bank and stopped. He sheathed his knife and held out his hand and walked toward the goat as if it were a dog. The goat nudged it with its nose and then began nibbling the cuff of his shirt. "That ain't for you." He pulled away his hand and attempted to pat the goat's head but the goat would not have it. As it walked off it tried to pull itself free of the hobble and it did not go far. "Betting it'd be easier for you to get home if you were free of that contraption." He knelt down to unbuckle the hobble. The goat took a few steps and he followed on his knees. "Quit your fussing." He grouped the buckles on the goat's front leg and sat back in the sand. "Go on. Get home." The goat stood there. "Suit yourself."

Toward dusk the air turned cool as if it were about to storm. He gathered up his things. The dead child's trunk was among them. He had not thought of himself as the stealing kind, but he was on his own now and with little money, and he decided it wasn't stealing if no one could speak against it. The goat had wandered off, but as he was leaving to find shelter it returned and followed him down the river path. He cussed and threw small stones at the goat and still it came. He stood with his hands on his hips. "You're a stubborn one ain't ye?" He then turned and bolted down the path and he ran until he came to some heavy grass and hid. Sweat ran down the bridge of his nose and he held his breath and listened for the goat. It came at a slow trot and its hooves thudded in the sand. The goat stopped when it came to the place where he had left the path. He looked up from his hiding place. The goat was standing above him, grinding a mouthful of grass.

The sky was low and black and thick with stars. Travel was slow. He had tried to get the goat to lead them, but it would not and he fumbled through the dark while the goat alternately fed and followed him. Not until late in the night did the moon rise and the sandy path glow with its light. Ahead the river forked and fell away and bats dipped and flittered against the sky like windblown bits of dark. The path rose up a steep slope of scree and when he reached its peak he sat and rested. Midway down the slope the goat had stopped and except for its pale horns and bell that caught the light, it seemed to be made of the night itself. Islands of shadow jutted in the distance. The calls of birds that did not sleep. Goat snorts. Then the faint sounds of voices. Laughter.

He followed the path across a bluff of sandstone until he came to a gully. Sparks rose through a canopy of cottonwoods and he saw people moving around a fire and he heard them talking. A woman and a man. Sagebrush and tufts of cheatgrass helped slow his descent down the path. Covered with dust and sweat, he walked out of the trees looking like some phantasmal greenhorn and when the goat appeared behind him no less unreal, the man seated at the fire rose and took up his shotgun. He looked at the goat.

"What are you aiming to do with that goat?" The man held his shotgun at his hip and the woman stood and walked into the shadows toward the river.

"Nothing. Ain't mine. You all want it?" the younger man stepped back and raised his hands to his hips.

"Hell no. Ain't yours to give, ain't ours to want. That hobble didn't get there by itself." The man glanced toward the river and then stepped across the fire. His back to the flames. "What's your name?"

"Preston Wood."

"Preston," the man said, as if weighing the rightness of the name. "You unloose that hobble?" The man pointed with his shotgun.

Preston looked at the goat then back at the man.

"No I didn't," he lied. "I found him that way a couple miles back. Been trying to get rid of him since."

"That the gospel truth?"

"It is."

The man turned toward the river and the woman walked up the bank and tied the goat to a tree. Behind her stood a young girl who Preston guessed was about 17 and a little boy who was naked and pot bellied and wet with river water. The man spoke to woman. "It's alright. Bring them up."

The woman walked the child to the fire and sat him down on a blanket and she brushed out his hair while the girl dried and dressed him. Preston watched her. The man lowered his shotgun.

"That goat belongs to a friend of mine." He walked over to the goat and laid his hand the goat's back. "He's been known to wander. Never this far, though. Hobble's to blame for that. Whoever loosed it."

"I reckon so," Preston agreed. He scraped the dust from the corners of his mouth.

"Well. Guess there ain't nothing to do about it tonight.

I'll have to ride him out there tomorrow is all. Come sit down."

"Thank you." Preston eased off his pack and sat and the man leaned his shotgun against a tree and joined him.

"Name's Ben. My wife Mary. Sara, my daughter. And this youngster's Jasper, my son." Ben took the boy into his lap. "The wife calls him 'the baby.' You seen any eight-year-old babies other?"

"Can't say that I have."

"Didn't think so." Ben lifted and set the boy on his feet and he walked to his mother and sat on her blanket by the fire.

"You taken your supper yet?" Ben asked.

"I ate a while back." Preston watched the girl prepare plates of food. She did so with one hand and held back her dark hair with the other.

"Ain't exactly what you'd call a Christian meal, but it ain't hunger neither," Ben said. "You're welcome to take it with us."

"I don't want to put you out none." Preston looked at Mary.

"We have plenty," she said. "Sara, fetch those pan-fish, please."

Sara rose and walked down to the river and Mary whispered in the little boy's ear. He walked quickly out of the fire's light and when he returned he carried a pan that he gave to his mother.

"Not that it's any of my business, but where's your horse, son?" Ben placed the fish in the pan so that they appeared to chase each other's tails. "I don't know how far you're fixing to get in this country without one."

"I don't got no horse." Preston rubbed his stubble. "And I don't know that I'd like one anyhow." He looked down at the cooking fish. They snapped and popped. Looked like swimming ashes. "I reckon I like to do things on my own steam."

Sara handed him a plate across the fire.

"Thank you."

"Welcome," she said.

"You come by train then?" Ben asked.

"Yes sir. By way of Mullinville. Been footing it since." Preston ate a piece of food and looked at Mary. "This is awfully good, ma'am. I thank you for it."

She looked at Ben and then at him and half-smiled.

"I've heard them called iron horses, but horses are made of flesh and bone. Like a man." Ben stared at his horses. "I don't see the use of such comparisons."

"I ain't much thought about it, I guess." Preston used a piece of bread to wipe what remained on his plate and when it was empty he set it beside him. He chewed his food and looked up at the stars that blinked through the cottonwoods.

Ben studied him.

"Seems to me you take from hell and put it here when you call a thing what it's not." Ben spat into the fire and without looking at Mary, he handed her his plate. "One hell's enough, if a man be of the opinion that there is such a place." Ben stared at Preston with a smile on his face and he did not blink.

Preston looked over each shoulder and then up at the night as if to judge the hour. No one spoke. The horses whinnied in the dark. The boy skewered a fish through its mouth with a branch he had whittled and he held it up in the light and peeled away its charred skin in strips and ate the meat with his fingers.

"Well, I'd best be getting on." Preston rose and walked to his pack.

Mary scooped the food they had not eaten onto one plate and covered it with another and she and Sara and the boy gathered what remained of the dishes and took them down to the river.

"It's fixing to storm, son. Why not stay on till morning?" Ben stood and looked up at the sky. "Can't see the stars anymore."

"I don't know." Preston lifted his pack onto his back and took a step toward the fire.

"Rain'll catch you. Pin you down in the scrub. Maybe worse." Ben knelt and stoked the fire. "But I reckon if you got to git you got to git."

Sara walked up from the river with some dishes and she placed them in a sack. She wore a cotton dress and when she passed before the fire Preston could see the outlines of her legs and buttocks. She looked at him. He looked at his boots.

Ben loaded his pipe and smoked.

"Beyond the fact of rain, I'd be lying if I said I couldn't use your help for a spell. I could pay you out with food and a little money. Make it worth your trouble."

Preston thumbed the straps of his pack.

"I'd like to think on it some. You mind if I give ye my answer in the morning?"

That night a heavy wind gusted through the trees and it smelled of rain that fell up country. Dead and living leaves whirled in the air. Coals winked in the ashes. Preston awoke to yelling and lightning. Spooking horses. Rain. Like competing nightmares. He pulled his blanket over his head and squinted in the dust. Ben held his two horses by the reins and spoke to them in some animal tongue while his daughter tried to calm them. The male bucked and reared. Legs and hooves lashing. Huge stomach heaving in the dark. Ben yelled to let him go and he pulled his daughter behind him and shoved off the horse. The horse disappeared in the darkness. Then the sound of the horse.

They got the mare settled and Ben asked Sara if she were alright and when she nodded he told her to check on Mary and the boy and then get on back to bed. But she stood and looked for the horse. "Go on," he said. "We'll tend to it in the morning." After she had gone, Ben walked up the gully and whistled. Preston watched. He whistled again. Nothing came but rain.

Seth was still drunk when they got to the mine and he prodded and spoke obscenities to JD. Kicked dust on his boots. Garvey studied the ground outside the mine's opening. Boards and brush lay thrown to one side of the tailing and the dirt was ringed and peppered with mule tracks and droppings. Garvey took off a glove and with his fingers he brushed away the loose dirt from a boot print.

"What you got there Garvey?" Seth asked, squatting beside Garvey and studying the print.

"A boot print. Damn mules obliterated every other." Garvey glanced at JD. Seth did too and he then picked up a mule turd and threw it at him. It made a thud and exploded against his neck.

"What the hell is wrong with you?" JD walked toward Seth, rubbing his neck and shaking the bits of dropping from his collar. Seth rose. Fingers wagging, then curling into fists. Laughing. JD stopped and looked down at Garvey.

"I ain't got any control over those mules, Garvey. What they do and what they don't. Don't be making that my responsibility." JD turned back to Seth.

"You're a son of a bitch," JD said.

Seth spat and tipped back his hat.

"Maybe I am, but you're a murrrrrderrrrrin' son of a bitch, JD." Seth studied JD, and when he got no immediate reaction, he went on. "I know that you killed them folks. And a child, for Christ's sake. You're going to burn for that one, son."

JD stepped closer until the rim of his hat touched Seth's brow. "Don't make a bit of difference what you call me. Besides, that bug eater had it coming."

The two men looked at one another for a moment and then Seth chested JD and shoved him. Garvey rose and got between them. He looked from man to man.

"Are we going to figure this out or ain't we?"

They crawled into the mine through a narrow opening. The smell of deep earth. Sulfur. Seepage. Must and guano. Garvey lit a match and found and lit a lamp. He held it while Seth and JD lit their own and together they walked down a trail of boards that sank and sucked in the muddy mine floor. They stopped at an interstice. The walls there shined with water and guano and flecks of pyrite. Garvey swung his lamp around and Seth slipped by him. Crate slats lay broken at his feet. He looked in.

"Well? What that sumbitch take?" Garvey asked. He stepped in and looked over Seth's shoulder. Seth pulled away the cloth packing that separated the layers of goods and when he judged the second layer to be undisturbed he laid it back down.

"Figurines. Set of cups." Seth turned to Garvey. "That museum feller know about them?"

"Which figurines?" Garvey asked.

"The set."

"With the animals?"

"Yeah."

"Damn it all," Garvey said, rubbing his jaw.

"I know it."

JD had gone ahead and he called to them from deep in the mine. The corridor opened onto an enormous cavern. At its center a deep and gaping shaft. Corridors leading off in all directions. Spoking the darkness. Worked lodes of silver arced and crisscrossed high above. On the walls some long-gone miner's cautionary scrawls. Cold blessings. Seth and Garvey walked toward JD.

"Stay to the wall," Seth said. He crossed a thin bridge of rock and once on the other side he waited for Garvey. "Damn shaft opens a hole in me every time I see it. Like I'm catching breath that ain't been knocked out of me." Seth held out his lamp.

"Quit your talking and walk." Garvey said.

JD's lamp burned brightly, and when he turned a jar made of dark clay in its light, Garvey stopped and gazed.

"Those them hands?" he asked.

JD placed the jar carefully in the crate.

"Yeah. Watch the floor."

Broken jars and their contents lay on the ground. Trade beads. Cups and jewelry. Tools, pots, and arrow heads. Some ancient's heart stuffed in a canopic jar and packed in red sand.

"Ah Christ." Garvey put his lamp down and sat against the wall.

"I'd advise you not to sit just yet, Garvey." Seth stood on the opposite side of the shaft. He motioned with his lamp. "Come take a look."

Garvey threw a stone down the shaft and cussed.

"Don't tell me there's more," he said. After a moment, he eased himself up and looked at JD. "Get these things back in the crate."

"Why me? You're right there," JD said, defiantly.

"Why not you?" Garvey was sweating and breathing heavily.

"It's not my damn mess is why not."

"It's not mine neither," Garvey's voice rose. "God damn your ass. You just do what I say. Man alive. What I tell you earlier?"

JD thought for a moment.

"That you'd take care of it. . ."

"That I'd take care of it. That's right. Now get that stuff up." Garvey worked his way along the wall.

Seth was kneeling beside a mummified corpse. A long dead warrior with sparse jet hair. Skin the color of shale. His mouth open and agape. Howling.

Garvey saw it and hurled his lamp in anger and it set the wall ablaze with oil. A few bats screamed and flew from their crevices.

"Son of a bitch. Where's the other? The big one?"

"Gone. Damn it, Garvey. You smoked us out. Shit." Seth rose and he guided Garvey down the corridor, passed JD, and exited the mine. JD followed. They sat beneath a mesquite tree and shielded their eyes.

"How about a cut of your chaw, Garvey."

Still huffing, Garvey slipped the block of tobacco from his shirt pocket and tossed it to Seth, who bit off a piece and waved what remained at JD. Then he threw back the block to Garvey.

"Suppose we go back to them mounds and dig ourselves up anothern?" Seth said.

"That's assuming there is another," Garvey said.

"You tell them you had two for them?" JD asked, as he took a drink from his canteen.

"Bought and paid for."

"Well, might make more sense to recover the one that was taken."

"Didn't you say that feller was on foot?" Seth asked.

"When I saw him he was on foot, but that don't mean there wasn't no horse." Garvey stuffed the tobacco into his shirt pocket.

"Doesn't mean there was." Seth spat.

"Either way, he's only a couple days gone."

The three of them sat without speaking. Cicadas ran their shrill motors in the branches. A breeze and the smell of sun-baked earth. Waves of heat. The far off tink of sledgehammers. Voices. Garvey moved his lips as if he were speaking but no sound came. He flicked his wad of chew on the ground. Stood. Dusted himself off and walked toward the mine. Seth stared after him.

"Where you going? We got to ready what ain't been took 'fore we go hunting anybody."

Garvey stopped but he did not turn.

"Tom won't be pulling out until late tonight. We'll drink some whiskey with him and give him what we have. Then we send him on his way. By the time he gets where he's going and the boys over at the museum realize what's missing, we'll have sorted out this mess. It'll give us time to right some things."

Seth nodded and hung his head beneath his legs and spat. Then he looked at JD. A grasshopper struggled between his fingers. He had torn off its wings and laid it on its back in the sand. It went around in circles. He watched and smiled with his tongue out.

Seth rose.

"That it will."

On the night JD would murder the travelers, he, Seth, and Garvey were riding in from the burial mounds and their mules were loaded with their take, including two corpses dressed in ceremonial garb and wrapped in burlap. Just risen behind a sky of dust, the gold moon glowed on the edge of the world and to the west pockets of storm drifted down country. The man was staring out across the mesa when he saw them. The robbers were silhouetted against the silent flare-ups of lightning. Garvey and Seth were out in front and JD trailed three pack mules. The man turned and walked toward his wife and daughter seated at the fire and he told the woman to put herself between the fire and riders and to douse the flames. But it was too late. The pair rode wide of them, but JD rode toward the fire.

The man could hear Garvey and Seth swearing at JD in hoarse whispers. Still JD came. He tied his horse on the outskirts of their camp. The mules stood frozen. The man watched as JD approached. Then he looked at the pair. They had doubled back and were coming at a trot. He spoke again to his wife and daughter in a tongue born thousands of miles away and the woman looked at him wildly. She pulled her daughter up and together they gathered their things. He spoke to her again and she slowed. JD stood there. Staring at them.

"Evening to you," he said.

The woman and girl stopped packing.

"You all mind if I join you?"

No one spoke. The man glanced at his family and when he turned back to the rider he saw the pair sitting their horses behind him. One of them called out.

"What the hell are you doing?"

"I was hoping to get some supper out these folks. Ain't that right mister? You're a coolie, ain't ye?"

The man looked at his family and back at the riders. His face expressionless.

"I don't give a good goddamn," Garvey said from the edge of the camp. "That sumbitch don't understand a word yer saying anyhow. Now let's get on 'fore he sees anything he ain't already." He turned his horse.

JD knelt by the fire and watched the woman.

"You go ahead. I'll be along."

Seth rode up into the light.

"You best mount up before we have ourselves a problem."

"We already there, Seth."

Seth shook his head and spat.

"The hell we are. . .you're on your own." He turned his horse and untied the mules and led them out into the darkness. "Yer a damn fool," he said. Garvey followed. But he turned and looked at the family. Their fire had been low, but buttons on the girl's coat held the light and that right there was enough to give them away. Then he looked at their faces and they were afraid and he was troubled by what he saw. As though he were looking at the oldest night.

After his companions had gone, JD walked around to where the woman crouched by the fire. She saw him coming and with a look she got her daughter up and walking toward her father. The rider knelt down beside the woman and poked through the bundle of things she had gathered. "What ya got in here, Mom?" He took her chin in his hand and turned her face toward him. "You don't need to be putting nothing up on account of me," he said. She turned away. A strand of her dark hair fell down across her face and she appeared both beautiful and utterly inaccessible. He took the strand between his fingers and slowly pulled until again she faced him. "And I mean nothing." The man and the girl looked on. Mute and stone-still. JD looked at them each in turn. Then he leaned back on one elbow. Crossed his legs at the ankle. "That true, mister? You all don't understand a word I'm saying?"

The man's eyes narrowed. He looked down at his daughter. Then back at JD. The woman collected herself.

"You see, it's fine if you don't, but that feller who just rode out a here, well, he thinks he's got you figured. And I'd like to prove him otherwise." He spat. His sunburned cheeks glowed over their bones in the firelight. The fire hissed and popped. The horse shook itself out. Its tack clinked. He grabbed the woman by the wrist and pulled her toward him. Wide-eyed, she looked at her husband and tried to fend off her attacker. Their daughter screamed. Cat-like and weaponless, the man leapt across the fire and he tore at the rider's embrace. The woman kicked herself free and got to her feet and she scooped up her daughter and the two of them ran into the night. The men broke apart. JD sucked at the air, wheezing.

"God damn you, mister. You better make yourself scarce." JD rose and moved toward his horse. The man looked for his daughter and his wife in all that dark and when he saw that they were gone he turned back to face the rider. . .

A blast of smoke. The shot hit him square in the chest and blew him backward into the fire. His dead eyes open onto the stars. "You little son of a bitch." JD left him to burn and he mounted his horse and rode for the woman and the girl. At his approach they tried to hide but he saw them and he caught them down in a draw. The woman spoke to her daughter and sent her toward the river to hide and she herself ran in the opposite direction. The rider watched them from his horse. He leveled his rifle. Aimed and fired. The woman crashed to the earth. Behind him the girl's shrill scream.

He rode down the draw and through the reeds along the river to flush her out. Moonlight slicked the water. The horse sank and sucked in the mud and its chest and rump shined with sweat. "Now where you gone to, a little darkie like you in all this night?" He looked from side to side and seeing nothing he rode the horse out into the water to its shoulders. There he turned the animal and watched the shore. Something moved in the grass. The horse snorted and its ears pricked. JD clicked twice with his tongue and worked shoreward. Again he stopped. Below him the girl was floating belly down in the water, clinging to reeds that grew along the bank. He bent over the horse's neck. "Look at me."

She looked into the horse's nostrils and felt its breath on her face and in her mouth. He turned the rifle in his hands and held it by the top of the still-warm barrel. The horse bent to drink and he brought the butt of the gun down hard on the back of her skull. A coyote yapped somewhere off to the south. Then another. The reeds slipped through her hands and she began to float down river. Bullfrogs croaked and crickets sang in the gold and wind-leveled weeds. The river curved away and after the girl had floated out of sight, he rode up the draw to where the woman had fallen. She lay sprawled and lightly steaming like some just-born island. He roped her to the pommel of his saddle and dragged her out of sight.

Back at the camp, he found the man still burning. And the charred smell of him. He pulled him into a patch of creosote. Behind an outcrop of volcanic rock on the camp's edge he found their mule and bundled goods. He cut loose the mule and smacked its rump. It kicked and walked a little ways and stopped. "You awnry sumbitch." He drew his knife and cut the drawstring of each bundle. In one bundle there were clothes and shoes. Dried fish. Porcelain bowls. Toys. Rugs and blankets. In another an axe and hammers. Chisels and mining pans. Shovels and a saw. The third bundle contained trinkets and fineries. Frail papers. Pictures and frameless portraits.

He took one portrait from the bundle and held it to the light. The dispatched family is standing on a pier. A freight-liner looms in the background and back of that the wide open sea. The water is rumpled and crested with foam. The man gestures toward the camera. His mouth is open. He and the woman have a hand on each of the girl's shoulders. Wind is blowing the woman's hair across her face. Her free hand gathers much of it. Gulls are perched and flying behind them. The girl is looking away. Her face is bathed in shadow. She is staring into the invisible, star-ridden sky.

The river had carried her to its southern bank and there she lay among drift wood and tumble weed. Feathers of crow and heron. A sun-whitened snake twisted and bloated in the branches. Blood leaked from her ears. As she dragged herself onto land, she had tremors in her arms. Fits of vomiting. She rested beneath a small cliff of sand and shivered in the night air. Down river some animal had come to drink and she could hear it lapping. Then it circled and stopped in the brush above her. She stared at the moon and spoke her mother's and father's names. As if she were summoning them to their final meeting place beneath another sky.

A cardinal called in a mesquite tree above the camp and with each bounce he shook drops of water from its branches. Preston sat up. His sopping-wet blanket fell to the ground. The little boy was sitting on a blanket, looking at him.

"Reep reep," the boy said.

Preston scratched his head.

"Morning, Jasper," he said.

"Reep reep," the boy insisted.

Preston looked around and then back at the boy.

"Reep reep?"

The boy grinned and rose from his blanket. A breeze sent tails of smoke over the ground and Preston stood and waved the smoke from his face. The boy pointed to the cardinal.

"I get you now. I see him. Fiery little thing, ain't he?"

The boy furrowed his brow and farted and ran toward the river. The rain had made the ground a ruddy brown and it was flecked white with bits of washed shale. The camp was empty. Preston looked over to where the goat had been tied.

"Ben took him early this morning." Mary came out of the trees carrying bedding and rain gear over her shoulder. "There's some meat in that pan there if you're hungry. A little mashed corn if the baby didn't eat it all."

"Thank ye, ma'am. But I'm not sure just yet if I'll be staying with you all."

"Don't talk foolery. You go on and get some of that into you." She hung the rain gear from the stump of a broken branch and then called to her daughter. When she did not appear Mary looked at Preston.

"Here. Take up those corners and smooth it out there." She unraveled the bedding and tossed an end to Preston. "Alright now. Come give it here. Thank you."

"You reckon Ben'll be back soon?" Preston took up his own blanket, shook it, and hung it from a branch.

"He'll be gone a while yet. You seen the baby?"

"Yes ma'am. I believe he's at the river."

Mary walked down the bank to the water. She returned

with the boy and his sister. They were wet and their legs glistened with sand.

"Fetch that jug of water 'fore you go," Mary said to Sara. "Come here baby. What you got all over?" Mary brushed the sand from the boy's legs. "You hear me?"

"Yesm," Sara said.

"Check him good 'fore you get on him. Lord knows what trouble he's been in."

To her mother's suggestion, Sara raised a hand and started through the trees.

"Where's she going?" Preston asked.

Mary studied him.

"If you don't mind my asking."

Webs of ground spiders lay like silver kerchiefs in the prickly pear and the saguaro were dark green and swollen with the monsoonal rain. The sky was low and deep blue. When Sara saw that Preston was behind her she stopped. A mesa lay out ahead of them and she studied it for fissures large enough to hide the horse. On the ground were traces of the horse's rain-beaten prints. She looked back at Preston.

"Are you coming or ain't ya. Horse will be in Mexico by the time you get up here."

Preston scrambled up the gully.

"Your mama said you wouldn't mind if I came along. You thinking he's holing up in one of those canyons yonder?"

"That would be the logical conclusion."

When they reached the canyon they rested on a dune just outside the canyon's mouth. The sand there was rain-pocked and criss-crossed with the star-shaped tracks of birds and mice. Early risers. Far below, the smoke of their camp fire rose through the trees and the river looked like a road of black glass. In the breeze the tall flowers of century plants quaked and burned like match heads. Two buzzards made wide circles in the air. Their bald and ruby heads shining in the sun.

"Listen." Sara said as she closed her eyes and cocked her head.

"I don't hear nothing."

"Shhh. Hold your breath and listen."

Above the hum and whine of wind over stones and plants, a hissing like the sound of small snakes.

"What is it?" Preston exhaled.

"The cactus." Sara took the jug and drank, then passed it to Preston.

"The what?"

"Damn. You can't even hear what's said directly to you. The cactus, they're talking." Sara climbed up the dune into the canyon. Preston stood and brushed the damp sand from his pants. "Is she touched, Lord?" he asked under his breath.

The canyon wound and widened. In the packed sand were the horse's prints and turds and piss-hole. Broken vegetation. Sara had gone ahead. Her tracks ran along side the horse's and at times they would suddenly face down canyon or mince wildly. Preston frowned. When he finally caught up to her she raised her finger and pointed to the sunny and south facing wall. There the massive and exaggerated shadow of the horse spread across the stone like a freshly painted pictograph. She tossed a coil of rope to Preston.

"He won't give you any trouble. Just set that end around his neck while I check him." She walked around the corner, making whooshing and guttural sounds, the likes of which Preston had not heard in his life. He flushed.

"What's his name?" He asked.

Sara's shadow merged with the horse's.

"I can't hear you. Come up." She was wiping down the

horse's back and flanks and rump with a piece of coarse cloth.

"What do you call him?" Preston asked again, winded.

"Red. Why?"

"Well, for starters horses don't much care for me, and considering I'm about to put a rope around his neck, I figured I should have something to call him by I guess."

"Alright. Get to it then." She stepped back and studied the horse. As though curtseying, the horse bent and rubbed his nose on his foreleg. Preston watched. He gripped the rope. Sara looked at him.

"Just stay where he can see you. If you don't give him a reason not to like you, he won't." Sara rubbed the horse's nose and gums, knowing full well the horse was about as harmless as they come. "Come on now. We don't need him bolting on us."

Preston walked slowly toward Red. Rope in hand. Repeating the horse's name in a low, monotone voice.

"You're about to give him a reason. Preston, Preston, Preston, Preston. How do you like it?" She turned to the horse and made clicks and soft syllables; spoke in her animal tongue.

"Seems to me talk like that would be an offense just the same," Preston grinned.

"That is where you're wrong. I'm speaking mother tongue, rocks and grass and water, sounds a horse knows as well as you know the words I'm speaking to you now." Sara held out her hand for the rope and when Preston gave it to her she slipped it over the horse's head.

"You holding that end good and tight?" she asked.

"I am." One leg forward and one leg back, Preston coiled the rope twice around each hand and stood ready.

"You're asking to lose those. Where did you say you're from?"

"I didn't." Preston cocked one eyebrow. Sara one-upped him and raised her entire brow so that her forehead furrowed.

"Missouri," he admitted.

"Don't they have horses in Missouri?"

Preston shook his head and uncoiled the rope from around his hands. "Well, yes they do, as a matter of fact."

Sara knelt below the horse and she checked his forelegs and hooves for damage and trapped debris. Beads of sweat appeared on her nose and cheeks and she flicked them off with her finger. Preston stepped around the horse to get out of the sun and he startled a greater earless lizard, its skin flecked ruby. Bands of black and yellow and turquoise across its groin. It puffed itself up and then ran. Its ringed and whip-like tail waving high in the air.

"Well, aren't you full of piss and vinegar," he said.

Sara appeared under the horse's neck. She could see the lizard nestled into a crack in the canyon wall.

"You're talking to lizards now? There's hope for you yet."

A light wind blew down from the mesa and on it the smell of damp sage and dust and drying stone.

"You ever been kicked?" Preston sat on his heels in the shade. He caught a whiff of the sweet, faintly musky smell of groin sweat and he closed his legs. He held the rope in one hand and smoothed his stubble with the other.

Sara lifted and cradled each of the horse's rear legs and then she gripped and slid her hand down the rope toward Preston. When she reached him he let go altogether.

"Once."

"Whereabouts?"

Sara looked at him with squinted eyes. He picked at the stitching of his boots.

"Here," she said, as she laid her hand below her heart.

"Yeah?"

"Mmmhmm."

"Why'd he do that?"

"Red didn't kick me, a mare we had awhile back did."

"Why'd she do it, then?"

"I come up on her too quiet. I guess she figured me for something I wasn't. That and she was a little gone in the head anyway." Sara opened the jug and drank.

"That lay you up a good while?"

"Could have, but I saw her coming. By then it was too late, of course. But I was able to move some to the side. She still caught me pretty square. Sent me to the ground in a hurry."

"Damn," Preston said, scratching his head. "Was there lots of blood?"

"Not a drop. Didn't even break the skin."

"How in hell?"

"Broke some ribs, though. And you could say she branded me." Sara smiled. She untucked her shirt and rolled it up.

Preston looked away and back again. Just below her breast was a scar. It was silvery and deep and shaped like a giant thumbnail.

"Well. . . ." Preston said.

Sara grimaced and rolled down her shirt. Then she stood and bridled the horse. "We should get on back."

"Alright," Preston said

Sara motioned that he should go ahead and when they were clear of the dune at the canyon's mouth she mounted the horse and offered Preston her hand. He climbed on and looked down at the camp, which lay beneath the trees along the river that flowed a mile away. A warmish wind picked up from the south. "Looks like we might be in for another storm," Preston said. Sara looked at the dark piles of clouds and their tilting curtains of rain. When she didn't respond, Preston added: "We do have storms in Missouri."

"Imagine that," she said, and then she clicked her tongue and the three of them set out.

———⊶⊷———

The western horizon grew purple before him and cords of pink and crimson clouds ran its length. Ben turned in his saddle and looked back the way he had come. The wind shifted and he could smell the long wilted blooms of yucca that grew in the high country and the sweet mixture of sage and rabbit brush that lived in the lower. His horse whinnied and he patted its neck. "I know. We should be getting on. We spent too much time on that damn goat. But it was good to see old Kimball, wasn't it?" He scanned the country behind him one last time and put the horse forward.

Below him a vast plain. Overhead a hawk spiraled until it hung just above the ground. It perched atop a saguaro like a totemic symbol and appeared to watch nothing at all until it dove and rose again with a ground squirrel in its talons. That's when Ben saw the shawl of dust in the distance. And then horses and three riders. His vision was blurry with swelling and dust, and with the night already at their backs, the riders seemed to have merged into one.

When he got within a hundred yards of them he heard one man's drunken singing and he rode along a hill of scrub in hopes they would not see him. The land fell away in shelves and he had just got to the bottom of the first when a rider called to him from above.

"Hold up there, mister."

"Shit," Ben whispered. He then slowed the horse and

turned him in the direction of the riders.

"Come on up for a bit. Have a slug of whiskey," the lead rider said.

Ben resisted the temptation to glance in the direction of camp lest he alert the riders. Then he spat and turned the horse uphill.

"How you doing?" the rider asked, handing him the flask. It had the initials "JDT" stamped into it. Ben tipped the flask to the man offering it. Then he took a long pull and handed it back. The men watched his face for signs of revulsion, but Ben didn't flinch. He may as well have been drinking water.

"Doing good. How are you boys?"

The youngest man turned in his saddle and muttered some crack Ben could not make out.

"Seen better days, mister. I'd be a liar if I said I hadn't," the oldest man said in a voice gruff with dust and dehydration.

Ben nodded.

"Where you headed?" asked the older man.

"Down to the river," Ben said.

"You working down there?"

"No. A little fishing's all."

"You smokin em?"

"Some."

"You alone?"

Ben looked from man to man.

"What do you boys want?"

The rider with the flask leaned over and spat a mouthful of tobacco juice in front of Ben's horse, wiped his lips, and sat silently.

"Well, I'd best be getting back. . ."

When they did not reply, Ben bid them afternoon and turned his horse toward camp. His horse's hooves clacked on the broken plates of shale and Ben rode him down into a dried up wash. The riders watched him. One of them rocked in his saddle. Creak of leather. A few feet into the brush, Ben looked back through the leaves of cottonwoods and saw the men talking. The flask winked as they passed it between them. Mary stood in the center of camp. She held a Colt revolver at her side.

"Where's Sara and the baby?" Ben asked.

"Baby's hid. Sara's looking for the horse with Preston." The dark forms of horses slurred toward them through the trees, and when they appeared, the men they held were smiling.

———— ∞∞ ————

Sara knew the sound of her father's Colt as well as the sound of her own name. Its ability to destroy and set things right had made an impression. She'd witnessed it fired perhaps a dozen times over the course of her life and she could recount them all. The gun's explosive percussion and whatever it ruined were linked in her mind, but now there was only the far off roar of the gun that put a big hole in the desert silence and momentarily stopped her breathing.

She tightened her grip on the reins and prodded the big red equine into a full run. "Hang on!" she yelled. Preston made wide hands and clutched Sara's hips and then pressed his legs around the horse so that his boot tips curved along the animal's underside. The horse shat midstride and tore down the slope with speed terrible in its precision. "What are you going to do. . ." he asked, too late, the words pounded and lost in the churning of the horse's hooves cleaving the rock and sand.

When they got to within a quarter mile of camp, Sara slowed the horse and scrutinized the trees.

"Hold up," Preston urged. Even before the horse had come to a stop, Preston had slipped off.

"What are you doing?" Sara asked, her sweat cutting snail paths down her cheek and neck.

Preston took off each of his boots and emptied them.

"You play cards?" he asked, pulling on his boots.

"I don't have time for this," Sara growled, her dark brown eyes hard and wide.

"All I'm saying is that until we know what's going on we don't want to show our hand. If we both ride down there, we'll have lost any advantage. You give me enough time to get to the trees, then come down."

Sara looked down at the camp and studied it for movement.

"Okay, get going."

Preston made his way down the slope and once he neared the trees, he again took off his boots, this time for stealth, and gathered them in one hand. Then he slipped into the trees and became a shadow.

As Sara neared the edge of camp, she was deafened by the thunderclap of pistol fire. After the ringing in her ears had subsided, she heard the drunken laughter of men she did not know and she saw her mother standing with her back turned.

Garvey was the first to see Sara enter camp. His huge hands hung at his sides like beef steaks.

"And who might you be?" he asked.

Sara ignored the question and cut toward her mother, who stood with the sidearm trained on Garvey. A wisp of smoke trailed out the barrel. "You alright, Mama?"

Seth and JD sat with Ben between them and JD's pistol lay in his lap. A blue-red goose egg shined on Ben's forehead and a chunk of his hair had been pulled out and now appeared to sprout from his shoulder.

Mary looked at Sara without blinking and Sara knew to say nothing of Jasper, who was nowhere in evidence.

"Well now, Ben. It is Ben, isn't it? I don't think you said anything about a daughter." Garvey walked a few feet closer and stopped, rubbing his chin. His black hair slicked back and helmet-like except for a few wisps fallen forward. "No, I am sure. You didn't. I would have remembered mention of a daughter as pretty as this. What is your name, honey?" Garvey moved toward Sara and Ben rose and so did the dust.

"Sit down, mister." JD cocked the pistol and stuck it in Ben's stomach. Ben looked down and saw the big, dark cracks on JD's knuckles. When Ben hesitated, Seth said he was standing next to a man who was without conscience and that he had better sit down if he intended to keep his guts. Ben told Sara to stay by her mother and then he sat down.

The air was heavy with the odor of sulfur and the men's horses shook against the flies. Sara studied the scene and all the men were intact and she wondered what her mother had fired on.

"What's going on, Mama?"

Garvey stepped to the side and Sara saw the crater formed by the Colt's huge bullet.

"As you can see," Garvey said, "your Ma damn near shot off my foot with that cannon a hers. And then there's this." He held up his hat. "I'm pretty sure I'm not supposed to see the clouds floating by through my hat. Next time we get rain in this godforsaken country, my head is going to get wet. Then where will I be?"

The weight of the gun was taking its toll and the barrel dipped in Mary's hand.

"Looks like your arm's getting a bit tired, hon. Why don't

you just lay down the gun so we can talk? It won't take but a minute," Garvey said.

Just then Seth got up and stepped toward Mary.

"Better stay right where you are, mister." Mary used two hands now and sighted in Seth's head and pulled back the hammer. The horses' ears lay back at the sound. Seth stopped.

"You're out gunned, Mom," he said. "And we've got Dad over here. Once the two of you are gone, who is going to take care of your daughter?" Seth winked at Sara. "It's lose lose for you." He spat and the spittle gathered the dirt.

"He's right," Garvey said. "Put down the gun."

In the earlier melee, Ben had been disarmed and pistol whipped and now his shotgun was leaning against the tree behind Garvey. Preston noted the fact and within seconds he had devised a plan. He set down his boots and studied the shadowed ground for debris that would crack underfoot, and when he saw the way he would take, he set out. As he circled around, he came to some boulders that had sheered off the canyon wall long ago, and they were large enough to hide a man and that is what they now did. Preston was about to make his next move when he saw movement out of the corner of his eye.

A few yards off, Jasper was crouched behind another boulder, shivering. He must have been bathing at the time of the intrusion because he wore only a blanket and the rest of him was bare. Preston peered above the boulder and he could see Garvey's back and the tree against which the shotgun leaned. Jasper started to snivel and Preston looked firmly at him and pressed his finger to his lips. The space between the two boulders was strewn with fallen branches and dry leaves and Preston knew that was reason enough not to go to the boy. The boy could wait.

Preston then moved around the boulder and slipped wraith-like through the trees until he crouched just behind the tree in question. He could hear Garvey using his best English to reason with Mary, to persuade her to put down her weapon and was she out of her mind thinking she could take the three of them should it come to that? Mary then said she might not take the three of them, but she would most assuredly get Garvey and she doubted the world would miss him one bit. Then she added, "Maybe the dung flies will know you're gone," and Preston smiled.

Garvey laughed and at that moment Preston reached around, grabbed the shotgun, withdrew behind the tree and carefully opened the well-oiled breach. Once he saw the shell caps were devoid of chinks from the firing pin, he closed the breach. Then, with his back against the tree, he used his legs to push himself up. The trunk was smooth against his back.

The melancholy call of a canyon wren fell from somewhere high in the cliffs. The sand was cool on his feet. He fingered the triggers, opened and closed his hand on the grip, plotting and trying to keep his breathing under control. As a boy in Missouri, he had shot squab and rabbit. Now here he was, ready to put the cold barrel of the side-by-side to a man's head. He had thought ahead as far as he could, but he quit all that because all that really mattered now was whether he was prepared to kill a man.

In two strides Preston had made it to Garvey and planted the barrel in the basal nook of his skull. At the cold hardness of it, Garvey put up his hands and said, "Ho there!" Ten years earlier, the moment he felt the steel on him he would have spun around on the toe of his boot, slapped the barrel, and taken out the man who held it. Now he could not trust his speed. Those days were gone and on days like this he missed them.

"Move over." Preston pulled back the hammers and used the shotgun to prod Garvey to the right so that he now shielded him from the other assailants. He glanced at Sara and then at Mary and her face was tinged with uncertainty, as if she couldn't be sure this turn of events was for the better. JD stood and stretched his arm in the duel style and with the gun trained on Preston, he told Garvey he could take him.

"Tell your men to put down them guns, mister, or I'll cut you down where you stand," Preston said.

Over the course of his forty-some-odd years, Garvey had heard many threats on his life and he knew the odd deadness of the killing voice and he was listening for it now.

"What's your name, son?" Garvey asked.

Preston drove home the gun until Garvey's head fell forward. "Mister, I got nothing to lose by killing you. Tell them."

Garvey had heard enough and he told his men to disarm.

"God damn it, Garvey, I can take him. Like shooting a hawk off a fence post. Done it a hundred times." JD was shaking with excitement and desperation as he looked down the barrel of his gun, his mouth agape and his tongue working a deep crack in his lower lip.

Corporeal supplicants, mourning doves cooed dusky mating songs on the edge of camp. In the throes of his own human troubles, Garvey grew very stern, as if he knew he had one chance to deter JD's impetuousness and keep things from falling to either side of the razor's edge. In a grave voice, he had not spoken two words when the Colt resounded like a great clap of thunder. BOOM! All save two — shooter and target — shrunk and closed their eyes at that deleterious sound, and when they opened them again they saw that the world had changed form yet again in that most of JD's head was gone, blown into the trees. Days later a fox would happen by and lick the blood from the pale green, diamond-shaped leaves.

JD's body stood with arm outstretched and the gun in hand and no one dared rise on the chance it might still make good on JD's intentions. Then the body of John David Thatcher crumpled like a sack of meat bones. Mary swung the gun around so that now the hot smoking eye opened on Seth, whose heart and sphincter tightened at the sight. He was here for the drink and the women he could buy with what little money he made, and he told Mary that as if she cared and then he laid down his gun and cautiously stepped away from it, as if the gun had held the man and at any moment it could return to his hand.

Ben picked up the pistol and joined Mary and Sara across camp. "You okay?" he asked. Sara nodded and Ben gave her Seth's pistol. When Mary didn't respond, Ben put his hand on the back of her neck and felt the softness of her skin and silky strands of her sweat-soaked hair. How to explain the act of killing another human except to deduce the absence of one's right mind? And how to reckon the moral vacuum wrought by virtue of it? Having never killed a man, she would need time to find her way back to the living, each and every one a descendent of killers and a killer in waiting. In the quiet of his thoughts, Ben told her that he would be there for her when she did.

As darkness fell, Preston gathered material to make a small cooking fire while Ben and Sara broke camp. Dry lightning flashed and in its white-hot glare Seth and Garvey appeared hogtied to a tree. Then darkness again, and again another long flash and Mary sitting in the middle of camp, moonfaced and distant-eyed, the gun still in her hand, limp wrist, dangling between her legs, and the boy Jasper standing by her in uncomprehending silence.

The wind would rise suddenly and blow dust and black leaves through camp and there was no telling them from the bats that ushered in full dark. Preston called to the boy.

"Hey, little man, do you want to try your hand at lighting the fire?" The question came out of the dark. More lightning.

The boy looked at his mother, put his hand on her head, and then joined Preston by the fire ring.

"Okay," Preston said, "Here's the thing: I'm going to give you one match."

The boy knelt and wiped the dirt from his hands.

"Yes sir," he said.

Preston could see that the boy was in turmoil and his cheeks were ablaze even though the night was cool.

"Hey," Preston said. In the dark, the boy's face looked like a charcoal drawing, but when Preston heard him breathing, he knew he was now looking directly at him. "Your ma is going to be fine, understand?"

The boy looked away at some noise in the dark, a faint rustling, a mouse hunting beneath the leaves, and when the sound was gone he turned back.

"Yes sir," he said. "I guess I do."

Preston patted his pant and shirt pockets for his matches.

"Alright then," he said, knowing full well he had not addressed half the boy's calamity. Hell, he hadn't addressed half his own. This was not the first time he had witnessed violence to the bodies of men. When he was just fifteen he had seen the mill foreman's days end when a log he was yarding broke loose, hooked him under the skull, and severed his spinal cord.

And then in the summer of his eighteenth year, the evening sky had turned black and strange with storm and the lightning spread throughout it like cracks in the ice. He and his family had stood on the porch and marveled as the green-black clouds grew and spread out beyond the shimmering corn field. Who knows how long they would have sat by and wondered at the bolts and streamers had not that same lightning traveled some ten miles and set their barn ablaze?

Preston's father ordered him to stay put and he ran down and swung open the doors, and cats they did not know they had — and mice they knew they did — ran out and pigeons with smoke in their wings flew from the hay loft. Preston could hear his father shouting at the animals as he freed them from their stalls. Once, he appeared in the doorway with the cow and Preston thanked God and that was his first mistake.

His father pulled his shirt over his face and went back into the heavy smoke to save the other animals and how could he have known that the flames would take him instead? Preston had seen his father devoured by fire. But a man's head disappear like spit in the wind? That he had not seen.

The boy heard a small dry sound when Preston slid out the drawer of wooden matches and took out one.

"Ever heard of the one-match rule?"

The boy said that he had not and he squatted there, waiting eagerly to light the fire.

"Well, you've got this one match and this one chance to light the fire. If you don't, it's my turn," Preston said.

The boy looked puzzled. "But don't you got a whole box of matches there?" he asked.

Preston smiled in the dark. "Yes I do, but that don't change the principle, and that is the need to treat each and every match as if it was your last."

A boy that age is not given to ideas that reside so far beyond the moment, nor to fathoming a stranger's principle. Far be it from him to believe in one match when a box of matches lay in front of him.

"Hey, how about some water over here?" Garvey asked. Preston looked for Ben and Sara and they were preparing to load the mule and saddle the horses. Mary hadn't moved.

"I'll get ye some in minute, now shut yer trap or I'll stuff a piece of burlap in there," Preston said.

Garvey mumbled a few words but the wind picked up and carried them backward into the night.

"So, the one match rule: You think you can do it?"

The boy said he would try, his wheat blond hair streaked black in places where it had not dried.

Preston had already built the foundation of the fire with dead grass and twigs, and when the boy put the match to it, it burst into flame. The boy quickly withdrew his hand and rubbed his knuckles where the fire had brushed them. Then the two of them fed the fire until it was knee high.

"That is a nice fire," Preston said, looking at the boy. But the boy's eyes were elsewhere. The firelight flickered and waned on the edge of camp and by its light the boy and Preston saw Mary standing over Garvey and Seth, head leaning to one side as she pondered the captives, tapping the pistol barrel against her leg as if she were reckoning the variables of some final calculus.

"Mama?" the boy asked, like a worried bird chirping in the dark.

"It's okay, just stay here and watch the fire. I'll get her." Preston rose and walked to Mary's side. She smelled like salt and soap and old fear.

Neither Garvey nor Seth said a word. They had seen her handiwork. The firelight lit the damp whites of their eyes.

Mary's face was shrouded by dark, so the two of them watched the pistol.

"Ma'am?" Preston swallowed hard and the sound surprised him. "Ma'am?" he said again.

Mary turned and looked at him and now half her face was illuminated. He had never stood this close and he saw an older version of Sara or was it her pain that made her beautiful?

"Yes," she said.

"Why don't ya come sit by the fire with me and the boy? We're going to get a little super going here before too long." Preston's lips were dry as leather and he licked them and then cleared the grit and stress sap from the corners of his mouth.

Mary looked back at the men tied to the tree.

"What about them?" she asked.

Preston looked for Ben and Sara, but they were loading the mule farther back in the trees.

"What about them?" he said. A great horned owl called from its perch atop a cottonwood and then alighted, the heavy whooshing sound of its four foot wingspan directly overhead.

"Who's going to make sure they don't get loose?" Mary asked.

"I will, ma'am."

She looked at him for a long moment.

"Alright," she said. "Take this." She put the pistol in his hand and closed her fingers around it.

"Thank you," he said.

Mary then joined the boy and put her arms around him.

Away from the fire, the night was cold and the cold climbed inside Preston's shirt and chilled his spine. He looked down at the two men, but he didn't see them. He saw his own mother and sister standing on the porch and waving goodbye. The cool breeze coming down the road and off the corn fields that whispered what Preston thought must be the indecipherable secrets of the Earth.

Seth looked around in stunned silence and again Garvey asked for water.

When Preston returned to the fire, Ben was putting on coffee and Sara was warming some beans and cornbread. When she saw Preston, she smiled at him knowingly and he turned away.

"Tough day, huh? Lordy me." Ben handed Preston a coffee cup and he sat down.

"Sweet hell," Preston said, shaking his head. "What are we going to do?"

"Well, we're going to eat this dinner and put some distance between us." Ben nodded toward the captives. "Then we'll do some figuring."

Preston nodded and held out his cup. The group ate very little and once the pans were washed and stowed, Mary, Sara, Preston, and the boy rode the horses through the trees.

After they had gone, Ben walked his mount over to the men and stuffed some greenbacks in Garvey's shirt pocket.

"That's for the dead man's horse and one of your mules," Ben said. "We'll leave the others tied down river."

Garvey sat up.

"Whereabouts?" he asked.

"Just follow the path." Ben motioned with his hand as if the place were right there.

"How we supposed to get loose?" Garvey asked. "These knots are so tight, I can't feel my hands anymore."

Ben knelt down and placed a small knife in Garvey's hand. Garvey thumbed the blade and it made a dull scraping sound.

"This knife ain't sharp. Take all night to cut through these damn knots."

Ben turned and led his horse to the trees where the others had gone.

"I'm counting on it," he said.

An hour later, Garvey was still sawing and the fire had burned down to coals and glowed there in the center of camp. Unknown to either man, a coyote appeared on the tree line, feet away from JD's body, which lay cold and crowned with a damp slick of blood. The coyote lifted his snout and worked the air for scent, the orange-red firelight streaking his coat and his nostrils flaring. He warily approached the body and stopped at the edge of plume that soaked the ground. He could hear the knife working and Garvey mumbling curses in the dark. When the men didn't rise, he sniffed the crusty stump, urinated on the body, and then returned to the sheltering dark.

⁓∞⁓

At dawn, the family made camp beneath the red cliffs that followed the river. Mary spoke with Jasper and Ben and Sara brushed out the horses and checked their shoeing and when that was done they hung bags of feed around their necks. Preston had ridden the dead man's horse, and as he tried to lift the horse's rear leg just as he had seen Sara do it, the horse banged him with his rump and Preston went down hard.

Ben, Mary, Sara, and Jasper all looked up and for the first time since he'd met them, their faces were uniformly amused. "Enjoying the show, I hope," Preston said, half-smiling and picking himself up from the dirt. He brushed off his pants and then leaned this way and that as if to realign his rattled bones. "The way I feel right now, you'd think I was damn near a hundred years old." Preston whacked his hat on his thigh, returned it to his head, and then he took a step toward the horse.

"Watch his ears and his tail," Ben said, but just then the horse swiveled in preparation to kick and Preston backed off.

71

Ben scooped a handful of feed from Red's bag and walked toward the dead man's horse. "Come here, Preston."

Preston walked wide of the horse, doubled back, and stood behind Ben.

"Take some of this." Ben eased some of the feed into Preston's hand and then stroked the horse's neck and offered him the feed. The horse snorted into his hand and half the feed scattered and what remained was gone in a single sweep of the horse's lips.

"Step up here," Ben said, and Preston took Ben's place and fed the horse.

"That's it," he said, scratching the horse's jaw. "I'm not all bad."

The horse cleaned Preston's hand and checked the other and when he found it was empty he put his nose to the ground and nibbled at the feed that had fallen there.

"Okay, we've got some figuring to do now," Ben said, and he put his hand on Preston's shoulder and the two men walked beneath the cliff, where they took seats and got to talking in the early morning sun.

"I'm pretty sure I saw that Garvey fella in town," Preston said. "He was there at the depot when I got off the train."

Ben listened as he rubbed Mary's shoulders. "What about the other two?" he asked.

"There was another man there with him, but I didn't get a look at him."

Ben nodded. "They ain't the law then?"

"Not that I could tell. Appears they might well be the opposite."

"Well," Ben said, "I guess we got that going for us."

Holding her knees, Sara rocked forward so she could see her father.

"What happened back there, Pa?" she asked.

"They accused us of stealing from them." Ben watched the horizon for any sign of riders. Then he spat. "Things went from bad to worse when they started going through your mother's things and I tried to stop them. The small man, Seth, grabbed me from behind and I was about to lay him out when the other one whacked me on the head. Damn near knocked me out. For a minute there I was wishing he would've."

Mary wetted a cloth with water from the canteen and dabbed Ben's goose egg. It was red and black and positively evil looking.

"That's when this one here shot off Garvey's hat. That was a hell of a shot, Mare." Ben laughed a little. "You'd think he'd seen the devil himself when he turned and saw Mary with the Colt trained on him."

Sara and the boy had drawn closer at the telling of the story, and they looked at their mother with a mixture of fear and admiration.

"Then the damn fool picked up his hat and made a move toward her. Don't know what he was thinking. And she about shot off his foot," Ben said.

Jasper wriggled in his mother's lap. "Damn fool," he mimicked, and then he blushed.

"Hey now," Sara gently scolded as she wiped a dead mosquito and its blood load from the boy's cheek.

"There was one other thing," Ben said. "The dead man had said something about. . .what'd he call them? Figurines."

Preston scratched his nose.

"You know anything about that?" Ben studied Preston so closely it was as if he were fixing to draw his face from memory.

"No sir, I don't."

The men locked eyes. Preston had played this game as

a boy and he had learned to switch off the chatter that went from his eyes to his brain and make the eyes that do not see. He had taken them, alright. Easy pickings. He had thought to sell them when he got to where he was going, but not a moment had passed since he had taken them and he was wishing he hadn't. He had looked at the figurines but once and then hid them away like a shameful secret and from then on he felt a strange coldness as if something planetary had broken out there in the world. There was nearness and farness to the feeling, and at times it seemed within range of his waking life; at others it was more like something he might have dreamed. Premonition or fever, he could not say.

"Well alright, then," Ben said, looking away. "We got to figure those men or the law or both will be hunting us soon, if they ain't already. Mom's going to be the one they want, and she's my charge." Ben paused here, knowing the words he was about to say were going to change all their lives and could not be taken back. "It makes no sense to risk them catching the lot of us."

Sara could see where the conversation was going and she stood up and paced, anger-and-sadness-tears welling in her eyes.

"Now hear me out," Ben said. "Mama and I will ride west." Ben looked at Preston. "And you, Jasper, and, hopefully, you, Preston will ride north. My brother Neff is a stone-cutter in the Heber Valley of Utah. He'll put you up and Mama and I will join you in the fall. What do you say, Preston? You got any place else you got to be?"

Preston looked at Sara and her face was pale and lovely. He could see her freckles then. He smiled at her and the boy.

"Well, sir, I wasn't looking for trouble but I sure did find it, didn't I?" He laughed. "You folks have been real good to me, and besides, I helped make this mess. So no, sir, I've got no place else to be."

Ben nodded and looked at the boy and Sara. "Alright."

The boy nodded and Sara welled over.

"The beginning of fall and not a day later, right?" she asked, wiping her nose with her sleeve.

"You can be sure of it."

Before the sun got too high, they divided the belongings and took a meal together. Ben drew a crude map showing the way to Heber Valley and he, Sara, and Preston discussed the deep swathes of pencil and upside down chevrons that signified rivers and mountains. They talked about where to find fresh water and fish and game that time of year and within minutes they had planned a month of their lives.

Monsoons had come to their part of the world and far out on the southern horizon a wall of dust three miles high rolled toward them. Behind that wall was thunder and lighting and drenching rain that would wash away the dirt and the blood. Ben looked into the darkening sky. A pair of turkey vultures rode the thermals.

"We're not dead yet, you sonsabitches," he said. Ben stepped to his horse, mounted, and offered his hand to Mary. The saddle creaked. She hugged and kissed Sara and Jasper and then she climbed up.

Preston pulled the Colt from his belt and offered it handle first to Ben.

"Hang on to it," Ben said, patting the shotgun's breach. "Mary and I will be fine."

Preston returned the gun to his belt.

"I'll take care of it," he said.

"That's one way of looking at it." Ben grinned and turned his horse west. "Best stay out of the washes. The face of the world is about to change."

———⊗⊗⊗———

Garvey shook his head in disgust and Seth rubbed his rope-burned wrists as they stood over the body. The coyote piss stank. Small cinder-orange butterflies had gathered around the stump and they dipped their lank probosces into pockets where the blood had not dried.

"Jesus H. Christ. So this is what it comes to." Garvey turned his back to the body and watched the river flow beyond the trees. It was the color of mercury.

"How do you want to handle this, Garvey?" Seth covered his nose and mouth with his handkerchief. "Do you want to get the horses and take him back to town?"

Garvey turned. "Do you want that stinking heap riding behind you?"

"Hell no."

"I didn't think so." Garvey said.

"Well what, then? Bury him?"

Garvey bent down and dug his hand into the dirt.

"Nah, damn critters will dig him up. Let's put him in the river."

The two men each took a leg and dragged the dead man's body to the river's edge. It was stiff as a board and as they pulled it, the stump plowed the earth, readied it for the planting of some fetid crop cultivated in hell or ancient nightmares. The water swirled and eddied back and cut a deep hole along the bank.

"I saw some rocks over yonder." Garvey pointed to where they had ridden into camp the day before.

"What are you going to do?" Seth asked.

"Get some rope."

They filled the dead man's shirt and coat with rocks and

then tied off each end of his torso so that the rocks would stay with the body. Seth wretched and dry heaved.

"Goddamit. Get yourself together," Garvey chided. He guessed the depth of the hole and tied a ten foot length of rope around the dead man's waist.

"What is that for?" Repulsed, Seth sat against a tree. Dirty face and ripped clothes.

"We don't want him getting away from us 'fore we know he's sunk. Rocks'll take him down and the rope will keep him there," Garvey said as he tied the other end of the rope to a thick tree root that the river had laid bare. "Otherwise, who knows where he'd end up. C'mon now. Help me roll him in."

Seth held his breath and bent down and he and Garvey rolled the body into the water. Posthumous baptism. They watched the rope go down with it until it went slack. Garvey gave it a quick tug and said "Good. Now get yourself cleaned up. We can't go into town looking all beat up." Garvey had dirt and blood spatter on his face and clothes.

"I hope you're going to take your own advice," Seth said. "If I didn't know any better, I'd say you were death warmed over."

They rode into town the next evening and before each man went his way, Garvey asked Seth to repeat what he was going to say if anyone asked about JD. He and Seth agreed this was unlikely since JD did not have a friend in this world, not even a dog, but sometimes when a dark thing dies another dark thing rises in its place and thus they could not be sure that JD's shadow would not come seeking the whereabouts of the once warm mass that had cast it.

"I know what to say, Garvey," Seth said, turning his horse down the side road to his place.

"Say it again, Seth," Garvey said to his back.

"I'm going home now, Garvey."

"Seth!"

"Go on home, Garvey."

Seth stabled his horse and then walked over to the bar to get a pint of whiskey before climbing the stairs to his room. A young, Mexican-Indian whore called to him from the road below and he could have used some affection, but he was covered in grime and stank and he was unwilling to speak the one or two words needed to make that happen. When he did not respond to her advances, she held her hands to the sky and cursed him with strange words and dance.

"You crazy bitch. Get on out of here before I shoot you dead." Seth had not killed anyone and he would not do so now, but it was the threat that people took seriously so he had learned to make it with conviction. She disappeared into the shadows, but he could still smell her perfume. Then he unlocked his door. When he pushed it open and stepped inside, the hot odor of burning hair fell out of the room just as the twilight was falling in, and where the slash of light ended Seth saw the bare feet of a giant red man.

"Who the hell are you?" Seth asked the darkness. As Seth watched, a fist four times the size of his own emerged, and when it opened, a human skull with long, jet black hair smiled at him from across the eons. Seth recognized it as one of those he, JD, and Garvey had stolen from an ancient burial site some months before. So large was the hand that held it, the skull looked like a child's, but it had belonged to a full grown man.

"Where did you get that?" Seth asked in a voice born of the wasted knowledge that the answers to some questions do not matter. The giant's other fist slid into the light and opened.

There in the center of it was Garvey's head. At the sight of that funhouse mirror of his face, Seth pissed his pants and fell backward into the cold womb of night.

PART THREE

Damn near a month to the day, Preston, Sara, and Jasper rode into Heber Valley with its thousand souls, many of whom were converts who had hailed from the motherland and from eastern continents. Like the Mormon brothers and sisters who preceded them, they were strangers to the valley, and to confront a strange land is also to confront the strangeness of the self. Thus their differences were not so great that—when threatened by the plants, animals, weather, and the dark complexion and earthen language of the first people to grow in that place—they would refuse to commingle and aggress with these Mormon moon crickets in their latter day mission to subdue the wilds and people the Earth and then be done with it.

Now the sun was slipping behind Mount Timpanogos, and when the sky went from blue haze to milky yellow, Preston pulled up his coat against the cool of the coming night and looked back at Sara and Jasper. Her face was ruddy from the weather and her sun-streaked hair lifted a little in the breeze. The boy's hands were locked around Sara's waist and they bobbed with the rhythm of the horse and Preston knew the boy must be sleeping.

The air was steeped with the sweet smell of just-cut hay that lay in mows on one side of the road and on the other barn swallows carved the heavy air above the river and snatched caddis and mayflies alike. Preston stood his horse and watched them while he waited for Sara and the boy, and did the world appear any better from up there? Climb a tree. Find out. All the while the far off clanking of a blacksmith's hammer divvied the silence and made audible the pulsing of the rubbish fires that burned high or low against the backdrop of the already dark eastern mountains.

Preston could hear Sara's horse coming up behind him and he turned the moment it reached him.

"Doing alright?" he asked, almost in a whisper.

The boy was slumped behind his sister and how he managed to sleep in that position was a rocking chair mystery.

"Yeah," she said, shivering.

A cricket sang in the grass just off the road. Then it stopped.

"You want to try to find your uncle tonight? Looks like there's a ranch house up ahead," Preston said. "I could go rap on their door."

Sara gazed at the river for too long.

"Hey," Preston said, "we can do it in the morning."

"Okay," she said, and they put the horses forward until they came to a path that led to an old Ute camp on the river. How long since they had been here? Preston wondered. He dismounted and tied off the dead man's horse. A fish jumped in the river and from the sound of it, it was sizeable.

Preston carefully removed the bedroll from behind the sleeping boy and laid it out next to the fire pit that was filled with ash. The boy mumbled something about pie when Preston took him down from the horse and carried him to the bedroll. "Sounds like a good dream," he whispered. He covered the boy and then made a small fire while Sara tended to the horses.

Another fish splashed and Preston walked down to the river's edge. Hundreds of caddis flies blanketed the river and the trout were gorging themselves. Across the river, a raccoon alternately washed and ate a large trout. When he saw Preston, he took the fish in his mouth and vanished into the trees. Sara came up from behind and put her chin on Preston's shoulder.

"How are the horses?" he asked.

"They need shoes, but they're happy to be eating fresh grass."

"I imagine they would be. You hungry?" he asked, feeling for her hand.

"I could eat a horse," she said, smiling.

The next morning, the boy awoke to heavy, shuffling footfalls and snorting. The sun was still a while from rising, but in the pale twilight he saw the lumbering forms of cows on their way to the meadow beyond their camp. Preston was the next to awaken. He peered out from under his blanket, hair all crazy and matted and morning eyes squinting at this least show of light.

"Sonsabitches have the whole valley and they've got to walk through our camp." He glanced at Sara and she was still asleep, so he disappeared under the blanket. "Go back to sleep," he said to the boy. "The sun's not even up yet."

"I can't," Jasper said.

Preston mumbled something in reply, but he did not stir. The boy dressed and used a stick to poke at the fire but it was dead as a doornail. He checked the horses and then grabbed their water pails and walked through the trees to the river.

Mist hung above the slack water and the boy's breath mixed with it the way night mixes with dreams. A beaver had piled gobs of mud and grass on the bank and willow branches stripped of bark lay scattered among the beaver turds on the river bottom. The boy had not eaten since noon of the day before and he felt that appalling hollowness as he looked back toward camp. Stillness. The mountains held pockets of slow melting snow on their northern faces, and even in July the river flowed smooth and heavy with runoff.

It was a fine sight. But then a crack of sunlight broke over the trees and lit the far side of the river, and reflected in that swathe of water the boy saw men and women and children and animals of all kinds and he knew that they had lived and died long ago. How they died was not apparent nor did it matter since knowing of no alternative to the sweetness of the Earth, every death is necessarily tragic, a notion that may itself be another mistake made by man.

On the bank above the swathe stood a Ute woman and her two children, a boy and a girl, and for a moment Jasper thought they were there in body, but then the breeze picked up and tore at them and he knew he was seeing more of the same. Suddenly he was sitting with them in a circle and the girl recounted the story of their deaths and the taking of their land while her mother looked on and her brother stroked an orphaned fox. She showed Jasper where the bullets had entered her body, as did the others. Even the fox had a hole in its side and all their wounds looked as fresh as the day they were made. She asked Jasper if his people were her killers and he said they were not. No matter, she said, since men who would destroy women and children would destroy all creation and this truth is written on the canine tableaux in the mouth of each and every man that was, is, or would ever be. Jasper was unsettled by this news and by the girl's voice because there was no judgment in it.

The pails clinked in the rising breeze and they startled Jasper, who seemed to sleep in this world and wake in another. He filled the pails and carried them through camp to the horses. Sara had been gathering wood in the trees and now she walked into camp with an armload and dumped it near the fire ring.

"What all we got to eat?" the boy asked, kneeling beside his sister as she organized the wood.

"Good morning to you, too," she said, pausing from her work.

"Good morning," Jasper said, averting his eyes.

Sara piled on some long dead grass and twigs and in short order she had the fire going. She had set two snares the night before and she went to check them while the boy built up the fire and boiled water for the last of their coffee.

The day was an hour older and the sounds of the valley drifted across it and two of those sounds were of Neff pulling on his thick leather gloves and clearing stones from his field. Preston had been awake since the cows walked through camp and he sat up and looked at the day.

"Morning," he said.

And the boy: "Morning."

"How about we get some coffee in us and then see if we can't catch some of those fish?"

The boy poked at the fire.

"Fire will be fine until Sara gets back," Preston reassured, pushing the wild hair out of his eyes.

The boy rose and brushed off his knees. He watched the flames and when the wind didn't bend them he said "Alright then" and handed Preston a mug of coffee.

When they got to the river, Preston found a section of cottonwood that had sheared off in a wind storm and he dragged it until it lay a few yards away from the river. "Have a seat," he said. "I'll find us some bait."

The sun was on the boy's shoulders and the day was warming up nicely and still he thought about what he had seen and about Ben and Mary and better days.

A dark fold of leather that had belonged to Ben lay flat on Jasper's lap and from it he took an oily coil of horsehair that stretched some twelve feet once he got it unraveled. Inside the fold there was a small leather sleeve that held stone weights and bone gorges of various sizes and he took the smallest stone and the midsize gorge, about an inch in length, and tapped his finger on either side, checking it for sharpness. A thin groove had been notched into the center of the gorge and he threaded the hair between his lips to moisten it and then he twice wrapped the hair around the notch and tied it off just as Ben had shown him.

The stone was shaped like an hourglass and he wrapped the hair around it and spat on the knot before he seated it. Then he looked into the water off the bank and he saw the shadows of fish, which he knew was exactly as good as seeing the fish. The trout hung about two feet off the bottom and with the twitch of a pectoral fin they would lift and rock from side-to-side for a fat nymph dislodged from the rocks.

"It's a good day for us and a bad day for the worms," Preston said, returning from finding bait. He had placed the worms in his shirt pocket and then covered them with dirt. "Here's ya a goodun." Preston handed down the deep red worm that dangled like an upside down question mark. "You're holding the king of the worms," he said. "He's the biggest of the bunch."

The boy held the worm next to the hook and, seeing that it was too big, he pinched it in half with his thumb and finger and handed up the remains to Preston.

"I could have given you a smaller one."

"That's alright," Jasper said. "They eat the same."

The worm shrank and writhed as the boy used it to wrap the gorge. Once the hook was covered, he stretched the surplus on each end and fastened it. When everything was done, the boy looked up at Preston and smiled.

"Looks real good," Preston said. "Now pop it in the water."

The boy slid off the log and went down on his knees and then his belly and he used his toes and elbow to inch his way to the water. He peered over the edge and saw the fish were directly below him so he eased the worm over and let it slide through his fingers and into the water.

"There ya go," Preston said. "Nice and easy."

When the boy had let out about six feet of line, he tightened his grip and waited. Preston sat very straight and tried to glimpse the line.

"Anything?"

The boy passed the line to his other hand and switched elbows.

"Not yet," and just then he felt a hard tug and the line go taut. When he was sure the fish was on, he pulled up and lodged the gorge in the trout's mouth. The trout tugged out into the fast water and the boy kept tension on the line as he let it out. Two feet. Three feet. Four feet.

"Ya got about two feet left," Preston said, stating the obvious. Finally, with one foot of line left, the trout stopped and held their side of the fast water. Fearing the trout would run again, instead of standing, the boy rose to his knees and started winding the line around his hand.

"That's a big fish," Preston whispered.

When Jasper pulled the line, the trout shook its head and again the boy waited. Slowly the big fish succumbed to the strain and drifted into the slow water and all the while the boy took in the slack. Then he worked the trout toward the bank and in one fluid motion he lifted the fish out of the water and it landed in his lap.

Preston made a sound of glee and wonder and he seized the trout and took it up by the throat. "My oh my," he said. The boy put away the tackle and washed his hands in the river and he felt as good at that moment as at any other time in his short life.

Preston and the boy could smell the sweet odor of cooking meat wafting through the trees and the saliva welled up in their mouths. Then they heard a man's voice and Preston broke into a run. The man's cattle dog ran to meet him but the man whistled him back, and when Preston reached the edge of camp the man said "Howdy" and touched the brim of his hat. Between them a rabbit reddened over the flames and its fur lay in a damp heap next to the fire ring.

"This is Mr. Allred, Preston. This is his land." Sara didn't smile, but she didn't look worried, either.

Preston walked around the fire and offered his hand.

"Preston Wood," he said. Allred's dog growled and stepped forward and he got him to heel and then the men shook hands. "We don't have two nickels," Preston said. "But I could work off the night's stay if you like."

Allred was thin as a beanstalk and his face was bronze and deeply furrowed and he had deep set, hard blue eyes. A grass stem swished side-to-side in his mouth. The boy came up behind Preston carrying the fish and he knelt by the fire and turned the spit. Allred watched him.

"You know what kind of fish you got there, son?"

The boy looked at the fish and then back at Allred.

"No sir."

"Well," Allred said, walking over to him and taking the fish by the tail and holding it up so the boy could see: "That's what we call a cutthroat." Allred used his finger to point out the deep red color beneath the trout's jaw that gave the fish its namesake. Then he gave the trout to the boy and explained how not ten years before, the Utes would camp and fish up and down the river during the spawn, and after they'd gone what few children there were in the valley would steal into camp and collect their beautifully crafted fishhooks, which were made from bone and raptor claws.

"They're all gone now, though," he said, looking into the trees as if remembering.

The boy looked over there with him and said, "No sir, they're not." He held what he could of the trout and took out his pocket knife and opened it.

"How's that?" Allred asked, amused.

Sara looked at Preston and Preston made the face that said he was hearing all this for the first time, too.

"You're talking about the people who lived here before you?"

"I am," Allred said, his amusement whetting into suspicion.

"A Ute woman and her two children were down river from me."

"Is that a fact?" the man asked, his gaze again returning to the trees.

"Yes sir, and the oldest child, a girl my age, told me what happened here."

Sara excused herself and walked over to the boy and put

her cheek against his forehead.

"Are you okay?" she asked, turning his face so she could look him in the eye.

"Some children got killed over there," he said, looking behind him, his mouth trembling.

Allred walked back to his horse and mounted it.

"You folks need to clear out," he said.

Then he stole a glance across the river as if this might be the end of days and he too would see the dead risen from their graves, the dark bullet holes in their bodies now the radiant and unseeing eyes of God.

———— ✦ ————

After they had finished the trout and eaten most of the rabbit, Sara stacked the bones beside the fire pit so the animals would find them. Jasper took the pail to the river and brought back water to douse the fire while Preston broke camp. Before things had gone south, Mr. Allred had told Sara to take the road north and that Neff's place was on the river just past the cemetery.

Sara and Preston led the horses out of the trees and onto the road while Jasper rode Red like some child king. White gnats hung in undulating balls above the fields, and the meadow larks sang from hidden places. The cemetery was built on a small rise and for a few minutes each day, the headstones reflected the sun. Three does were eating the wild grass that grew atop the graves and when the group passed below them they stopped, looked, and listened with their big black eyes and massive ears. The does had foraged alongside many horses in their day and they did not fear them, but they knew better than to linger at the sight of the shape of man, and one by one they jumped the small aspen fence and disappeared behind the hill.

A deeply rutted two track left the main road, and the three followed it until they came to a cabin chinked with mud and grass and bits of stone. Smoke rose from the chimney, but when they knocked on the door, no one answered. "Someone's around back," Jasper said, climbing down from the horse. They tied off the horses and followed a path worn through the waist high grass. The farther they walked, the louder the sounds became, until finally they saw a large man showering buck naked beneath a bucket of water.

He was heavily muscled and his face and neck and hands to the middle of his forearms were dark brown while the rest of him was milk white, dusty, and flecked with hay bits. A small towel and his clothes hung from nails driven into an aspen, and once he was finished washing he stepped out and took the towel and dried himself. Sara turned away at the sight of his prick and sack that hung between his legs like a weathered coin bag. Preston just smiled and the boy watched a lady bird inch its way up a blade of grass.

"Are you Neff Saunders, brother of Ben Saunders?" Preston asked. Neff kept his back to the voice and pulled on his trousers.

"Who's asking?" he said, turning around.

Preston told Sara it was okay to turn around and she did so and saw in Neff's face a vague resemblance to her father. Sara stepped forward and offered her hand.

"Hello Uncle Neff," she said.

Neff's hands were rough from handling stone and his fingers were thick and curled from grasping tools. "Well, I'll be," he said.

Sara started to explain why they had come, but Neff said

he pretty much already knew why but that she could fill in the details once they had gotten settled.

They sat outside and ate a late breakfast of eggs, coffee, and toast and once that was in them Preston and the boy agreed to help Neff clear and pile stones from the field and Sara said she would look after the horses and organize their belongings. She began to clear the dishes and Neff said they could wait.

Afternoon found her sitting beneath a tree with a cloth spread out in front of her, and atop that the Colt revolver emptied of rounds and a bore brush that she had used to clean the barrel. She sighted the gun and buffed it with a fresh cloth before returning the rounds to the cylinder. When she was just a girl, Ben had held a round between his thumb and finger and told her they were magical because they could make certain things disappear, and so far as anyone knew, these things would not be seen again. Though it is true the gun is man's most disgraceful invention, he said it is in the world to stay and the only counteraction is to respect it.

She pulled back the hammer until it locked and then she unlocked it and sat it. Out in the field, a large dust devil appeared and Neff and Preston turned their backs to it and waited for it to move on or die and die it did at the boy's feet.

The three quit work that evening and when they returned to the cabin, they found a note on the door from Sara that said she had gone to set some snares. Neff had managed to stay relatively clean, but Preston and the boy wore the sweat and filth of mountain days. Black moons of dirt lay beneath the boy's nails, and Preston's chest and stomach were streaked from where the sweat had cut paths through the heavy dust. Neff looked at them and said they were quite a pair. "Why don't you two get cleaned up and I'll put together some grub?"

Neff gave them the buckets and they walked down to the river and filled them.

The buckets were five gallons each and Jasper was having a hell of a time carrying his, so Preston asked him for it and the boy reluctantly set it on the ground. The boy's trousers were soaked from the sloshing water and Preston said he knew it had been awhile, but he was still sure that the boy was supposed to take off his clothes before bathing. The boy gave Preston a hard look and Preston smiled and picked up the bucket. When they reached the shower stall, Preston poured one of the buckets into the shower bucket and said the boy could go first.

"When you're ready, looks like you just slide out this plate here," Preston said, pointing to a tightly fitted sheet of tin that held back the water.

"Where do I undress?" Jasper asked meekly.

Preston looked around.

"Behind that bush, I reckon."

The boy shrugged and took off his shirt and then his shoes and pants, which he then hung from the nails in the aspen. The sun was right above the stall and Jasper was grateful for that because the water was cold and he huffed and washed vigorously.

"You still got dirt all over your back," Preston said. "And wash those ears. . . I can see the dirt on them from here. You and dirt partners or something?"

The boy scrubbed his ears and turned his back into the water.

"Did I get it?"

"Nope. It's still there."

"Where?"

"Right there."

"Here?"

"Nope. More to the left."

"Here?"

"A little bit lower."

"Now?"

Finally, Preston busted up laughing and the boy said "Damn it, Preston," and angrily slapped the plate and shut off the water.

That night Neff built a fire on the river and they all supped on potato soup while venison and wild onion roasted in a cast iron pot handed down through the generations. A breeze came out of the east, and when Neff poked at the coals, sparks rose and the breeze carried them to the darkness of the sliding water. Neff took his seat on a pine round, the last remnant of tree he had felled the fall before, and he looked at Preston and Sara and then at the boy, who was slurping a spoonful of soup.

"This is the best soup I ever had," Jasper said. Then he tipped up the bowl and drank. Old moon in the new moon's arms. He set the spoon and bowl aside and leaned forward and watched the fire.

"My mother used to make that soup," Neff said, using a stick to lift off the pot lid and turn the roast with his knife. "Ben never made it for you then?"

The boy shook his head and Sara said "No he didn't," and Preston watched the breeze lift the shirt away from Sara's breast so that just the edge of her aureole showed.

"So tell me, now, what are you running from?" Neff asked.

The night passed with Sara and Preston telling the story of their departure from the southern climes and Jasper nodding in somber agreement as the river caught the stars that wheeled overhead. Neff listened. His face was free of emotion. As if turning a man's head into mist were essentially indistinct from gutting a rabbit or shooting a deer. He served up the meat and it had been cooking for so long, it fell apart on the plate and the onions steamed atop it, and before anyone could say a word, the boy started shoveling the food into his mouth as though he were eating for the first time or attempting apotheosis.

Once Sara had told their story, she told Neff she understood if he wanted no part of it and that they would move on. Neff whipped the dregs from his coffee cup and set it atop his plate.

"Well, I appreciate that, Sara. But you needn't go anywhere." Neff smiled and again she saw her father in the details. "I wouldn't have asked you to tell me what happened if I weren't ready to live with the consequences. I just hope Mary and Ben are holding up alright. That is a hell of a heavy burden to carry." Neff looked up into the sky and then at the outlines of hills that were bathed in an ashen glow even though there was next to no light to speak of. He took a long, deep breath and then let it go. "Hard to imagine all the terrible things going on out there." Then Neff bent down and picked up the coffee pot and he offered it to each person.

"What did you do for work before you started wandering?" Neff asked Preston as he topped off his cup.

Preston scratched his head.

"I worked my family's corn farm for awhile. After that, let's see. I did a little carpentry, mostly around the house."

Neff offered the coffee to Sara but she waved it off.

"What did you do, fix chicken coops?" Sara laughed.

"Among other things," Preston said in his defense.

"Like what?" she asked, all teeth and youthful loveliness.

"Hell, I don't know. Just things. Barn door and what not. It's been a while," he said.

"You good with a hammer, then?" the older man asked.

Preston thought about it and said he supposed he was good enough.

"That's what I wanted to hear," Neff said. "I know a guy down the road who likely could use your help. He and one other guy — a kid about your age — are contracted to build half the town, damn near. How's that sound?"

Preston looked at Sara and she smiled and squeezed his hand.

"Good," he said. "But do you think I could borrow a hammer?"

"There's a trout behind that rock," Jasper said, plain as day. Sara, Preston, and Neff looked at him and they saw he had fallen asleep on a blanket near the fire.

"I'll tell you what, you could write a book with all the things he says in his sleep," Preston said, putting on another piece of wood.

Sara pushed the hair from Jasper's eyes and with it went the light sweat that glistened on his forehead.

"What happened out here with the Utes, Neff?" she asked.

The fire popped and sent an ember onto the boy's blanket and Preston snatched it up and flicked it back into the fire. The question threw Neff's face off balance.

"I'd only be telling you what I've heard rumored if you've got the stomach for it, but how do you know about any of that?"

Behind them to the north, a wetland bordered the river and hundreds of peeper frogs were singing out there in the dark and no wonder the boy had fallen asleep amidst that sweet monotony.

Sara peered into her coffee cup as if in the remains of that cold dark pool she would see the answer reflected as in some necromancer's glass.

"It's hard to explain," she said.

"You think what I've got to tell you isn't?" Neff patted his shirt pockets and from one he took a small wooden pipe and from the other he pulled a leather bag. Preston and Sara couldn't see what was in the bag, but when Neff opened it they wondered if a skunk were about. Neff held the bag and pinched off a bit of whatever was in there and stuffed it into his pipe.

"What you got there?" Preston asked.

"Oh, it goes by different names." Neff took a stick from the fire and put it to the bowl and drew and held. "Here," he said, handing the pipe to Preston. Neff blew the smoke into Preston's face.

"What kind of tobacco is that?"

"The good kind," Neff said, offering him the lighting stick.

Preston drew off the pipe and it sent him into a fit of coughing. Afraid he might wake the boy, he gave the pipe to Sara and got up and walked to the river's edge, where he could cough in peace. Sara sniffed the bowl and she could feel and smell the hot fragrance. Then she drew from the pipe and nearly started coughing herself.

"You were saying?" Neff said. Now that his face was calm, she could see he had white crow's feet from squinting in the sun, and the skin over his cheekbones was tight and brown like drum leather.

"Evening before last we camped on the river just past the cemetery." Sara looked around and oriented herself in the darkness until she had found the direction of the camp. "You know the place?"

"The fishing camp."

"Yes," she said. Her eyes were bright and glassy.

"I know it well." Neff tapped his pipe on a stone to clear the bowl and returned it to his pocket.

"Well, Jasper said some folks had been killed there. Children."

"Who told him that?" Neff asked.

"So it's true, then?"

Neff shook his head.

"Yes, it is, unfortunately." Neff thought for a moment. "But people have always killed and been killed damn near everyplace by now. The Earth isn't but one big grave."

"A Ute child told him," she said.

"Well I'm not sure how that could be. Utes haven't been seen in these parts for some time," Neff said.

Preston came up from the river and he was sopping wet.

"Fell in the damn river," he laughed. "Don't know how I managed it, but I did."

Neff got up and piled a couple big logs on the fire.

"There's a sawhorse yonder," he pointed at the back of the house. "Set it here and dry your clothes."

Preston stumbled away from the fire, his eyes blind with firelight. When he was gone, Sara turned back to Neff.

"I don't think he saw them like you're seeing me now," she said. She took a sip of cold coffee. "Maybe he dreamed it."

"Did your Ma or Pa ever tell you about your Grandma Lou's visions?" Neff asked.

"No sir, they didn't."

"Good old Lou. I was wondering when we were going to see her gift again."

Sara leaned toward the fire and held out her hands.

"Visions of what?" she asked.

"Different things, I suppose. Things that had happened, things that maybe were going to happen, and things that were happening that most people can't see."

Preston returned from the darkness carrying the sawhorse, which he set next to the fire. Neff threw him his blanket and as he undressed down to his underwear and then to nothing, he started in on the river and how cold it was and how slick the stones, and he would have gone on that like that had Sara not said "Can't it wait? We're talking about my Grandma Lou's visions?"

Preston stopped his tirade midstream.

"Visions?"

"That's right," she said.

Preston took his seat by the now high, bright fire. He was pretty sure he saw the faces of animals in the flames, but he kept that knowledge to himself.

Neff looked at the boy.

"Your Pa told me that when Lou was a girl, a little older than Jasper is now, she was asleep in her room and sometime in the early hours of the morning she was awakened by hushed voices and the sound of people walking."

"Whose voices were they?" Preston asked, serious as sin.

"Let him tell it," Sara said.

Preston cheeks were already flushed from the fire, but his face deepened by two shades of red.

Neff smiled at Preston and then continued.

"So the voices — she can't tell whose — but she hears people talking, so she starts to peer out and someone covers her head with the blanket so she can't see. Then the voice of whoever is holding the blanket over her head says not to be afraid. That they were just passing through and would soon be gone."

A log fell out of the fire and startled them all. Neff used a stick to roll it back into the pit.

"A couple minutes pass and sure enough, the room got quiet again. Lou gets out of bed and sees circles drawn around her bed posts. She told me she thought they were there to protect her, from what, she didn't know. She guessed her room was a door way or some such thing." Neff leaned back and looked at the stars winking in the milky blackness. "She lived 72 years with those far eyes, seeing what she saw, knowing what she knew. It wasn't easy, but she learned to live with it, and your brother will, too."

Sara awoke just as the sun was rising over the mountains. She, Preston, and Jasper shared a room that smelled of pine, and out its window black capped chickadees combed the chinking for seeds and insects. Preston slept deeply. He had spent a good part of the night and the early part of morning lying on his back wondering about ghosts and stars and the extent of the universe. She hadn't heard him carry on like that. She pulled the boy's blanket up to his shoulders and then she wrapped herself in her own blanket and walked into the kitchen to make coffee. She held her hand above the pot belly stove and, unsatisfied, she fed it the last two cuts of wood and pulled on her boots to bring in more.

Neff's cabin faced south and to the east were a wood pile, splitting stump, ax, and awl. Neff's garden was to the west and it was already glowing in the morning sunlight as Neff walked from plant to plant with a watering can. He wore a large, grass hat he had woven, and it bathed his face and shoulders in shade. Sara stacked the wood she had gathered and walked toward Neff.

"Morning," she called, raising a hand.

"Morning. Sleep well?" Neff put down the can and wiped his brow with a handkerchief.

"Well yes I did. Like a dog. What are you doing out here this early? You're up with the birds."

Neff stuffed the hanky in his back pocket and looked at his plants. "It's best to water before it gets too hot," he said.

Sara ran her hand along the top of the tomato plants, next to which grew four plants of a kind she had not seen before.

"What is this plant here?"

Neff went down on one knee and pulled a young bull thistle from the base of the tomato plant and shook the dirt from its root ball. He shifted and touched the leaves of the plant in question.

"A lovely plant, isn't it?"

"Yes," she said.

"A few years back, I did some stonework on the railroad down there in Provo Canyon — you came up that way, I believe — and I hurt my back. I thought I was done for. I really did. Well, word got around and this old Chinese laborer I had helped with some ties came calling and he gave me his pipe with this plant in it. He didn't speak any English, but I came to understand that whatever he was offering me would help with the pain."

Sara nodded and shielded the sun from her eyes.

"Is that what we smoked last night?"

"It is. But there is another reason I grow it. Look here." The plants were still small, but their long, slender leaves were sticky and swirled out from the plant where they trapped aphids, gnats, and other tiny insects as they motored through the air.

"It's a bug catcher?" Sara asked.

"That's right. Look closely, though."

Sara went down on a knee and studied the leaves.

"Is that pollen?"

Neff nodded.

"Best way to prevent cross-pollination, right there." The two stood there, admiring the plants and enjoying the warmth of the sun on their backs. "Come on," Neff said. "I have a surprise for you."

They followed a small path to the edge of the property. There deer turds steamed in the tangle of dead and living grass. In a grove of trees, a small, two room cabin had been erected some 20 years earlier by a mountain man who ran mink and beaver traps throughout the valley and the mountains to the east. Above it all, three crows mobbed a red-tailed hawk. The cabin door was hinged with the hide of some long dead ungulate and a thick nub of deer antler had been seated in a slot that kept the door closed. Neff removed the nub and dropped it in his pocket.

When he opened the door, a draft of cold air rolled out of the darkness. Neff entered the cabin while Sara waited outside. She heard things being moved and a moment later, Neff opened the heavy window cover in the front room and a large shaft of sunlight fell onto the cabin floor.

Sara stood in the room as Neff opened three more windows and the cabin flooded with the deep, golden light of early July. They walked from room to room. The cabin was sparsely furnished. A table and two chairs. A fireplace made of river rock and a mortar of mud, grass, and ash. In the bedroom, a raised bed and a small table by the window.

"Who lived here?" Sara asked.

Neff ran his hand along the cool, smooth head beam above the doorway.

"A fur trapper."

"Where is he now?"

"Right outside. See his headstone there?" Neff asked, peering through the window.

Sara looked outside.

"You mean that rock?"

"That would be it."

"That's too bad," she said.

"Well, people die."

"Did you bury him?"

"No, he was like that when I got here," Neff said. "Let me show you a couple other things."

The trapper had fashioned a cot that folded against the wall, and Neff showed Sara how to unlatch it and unfold its legs. Then the two walked outside and around the back. "That's the outhouse over there. But this is what I wanted to show you." Neff bent down and lifted a heavy oak door. "This is your cellar. Not sure why he dug it out here, but it works as well as any. I used it while I was digging my own."

Sara kneeled on the edge of the cellar and looked in.

"Did you say 'my' cellar?"

"You can stay here as long as it suits you."

Sara smiled.

"That may be a while," she said.

As they walked toward the garden, a foraging mouse crossed the path behind them and a bull snake pursued it into the dark, sunlit grass.

———— ❦ ————

By the end of July, Preston, Sara, and Jasper had settled into the trapper's cabin, and the days they spent there were among the finest they had lived. Preston worked for Pickard as an apprentice carpenter and were it not for Rance — Pickard's other apprentice, a young man who, as it happened, came from a town in Missouri that wasn't ten miles from where Preston had grown up — the work would have been equally steady and pleasant.

But the pay was good and there were the afternoons that cooled into evenings, which in turn deepened into nights by the fire, eating and talking and dreaming about the life they had and the life they still wanted, taking care to never appear as though the moment weren't the most precious thing between them. One night by the fire or a single afternoon spent walking in the hills with Sara and the boy obliterated whatever uneasiness Preston felt about people and the world beyond the known distance.

August came and went. Then September, and with it the turning leaves and frost on the grass and in the air plumes of wood smoke and great flocks of birds flying south with the approach of winter. Sara saw to the garden and readied the cabin for the cold months ahead. Throughout the day she stole glances down the road, but the first large flakes of snow had started to fall and still no sign of Ben and Mary or those that hunted them.

Twice each week Jasper would rise before dark and go to work with Preston, where he would sweep the sawdust and wood scrap into piles and convey it outside where they would burn it to keep warm. On one such occasion, he was warming his hands and face when Rance walked over and stood on the opposite side of the fire pit. Rance had shoulder length red hair and a heavy beard that hid most of his youthful face. "Nice fire," he said. Then he held out his hand above the flames: "I'm Rance." The boy looked at his hand and saw the dark red hair on his knuckles. "Take it," Rance said. "That would be the polite thing to do."

Jasper looked for Preston, but he was hammering somewhere in the building. A draft horse was hitched to a load of sandstone in front of the livery stable down the road, its breath clouding in the cold morning air. No one else was about. Jasper then reached across and shook Rance's hand and his mind filled with images of things he had never seen: A man stood in the middle of a frozen pond, surrounded by blue-black pines and low lying clouds that dropped a light snow, and there in front of him a black eye of open water where something had broken through the ice. And then a flash of light like a mirror catching the sun, and next he saw Sara bathing in the river and washing her supple breasts. Jasper wanted to look away, but he couldn't. He had no say. A yellow warbler alighted in the tree above the hiding eyes and Sara looked there, covered her breasts, and then the eyes fled.

Another burst like a match put to gun powder and now Rance's enraged face loomed above. Then Jasper saw his clenched teeth and the belt in his hand. Jasper felt his ears lay back and his body stiffen for the blow. Rance brought it down on his back and the boy heard a whelp of pain rise from deep in his body. He felt his sphincter loosen as a trickle of piss ran out onto the floor and pooled around the feet of the dog through whose eyes he now looked at the world, and he knew this dog was dead.

Jasper pulled away his hand and headed for the building. Rance watched him go. "What's wrong, boy? Fire get ya?" He found Preston working inside and he wanted to tell him all that he had seen, but he did not know how. Preston looked at the boy's face, and though it did not give specifics, it still said it all. "What's the matter?" he asked. But all the boy could muster was "Rance."

At this Preston put down his tools and held the boy by

the shoulders and he told him to steer clear of him always. Then he went outside and had words with Rance. The boy could see them through the window and Preston did most of the talking and he would point at the building and the two men would look in that direction as if they expected to see the boy there instead.

"I didn't say but three words to that boy," Rance said. He put his hands in his pockets. "And if I did, what is it to you? A man can't have a little polite conversation?"

"I'm not here to talk about what was said and what wasn't. I'm asking you to stay away from him."

"Fine by me," Rance said.

Preston turned and started for the building.

"Preston," Rance called.

Preston turned.

"Say 'hello' to Sara for me, will you? She sure is sweet. Did you know she ain't married yet?"

Preston and the boy rode to the house where Neff was working, and when he came out the three of them rode home together. They passed Mr. Allred on his way into town and Neff touched his hat and Allred hesitated and then did the same. The two men had had their share of hard words over the years, and even now their disagreements over the land and how to live on it hung between them like smoke in the air and these troubles would outlive them both.

In summer, Allred and his hands would drive several hundred head of cattle to their mountain feeding grounds where they would devour far more of their share of living things, from tender lupine to the loco weed that raked the bovine brain until its bearers starved or walked off a cliff or were lost outright, but not before aborting their twisted fetuses into the dust.

The men's properties abutted the river along which the cattle wandered most of the day and part of the night and the damage to it was entire. Ten years earlier, Neff had invited Allred to take a meal with him to discuss all he had seen and what might be done to curtail the destruction. After they had eaten, Neff got to talking and he very well may have said too much because Allred just sat there quietly and tapped his finger on his knee.

When Neff had spoken his piece, Allred's finger stopped tapping and he asked Neff what he was proposing he do. Neff offered him another piece of pie and Allred waved it off.

Allred's face looked stern then and the veins on either side of his neck rose and fell with each heart beat. Up to that time, he had practiced a detached civility toward Neff, as though he were being tolerated and nothing more, which is how it was with the Gentiles that could not be reached by the missionaries and the townspeople with their promises of heaven, eternal life and, in the meanwhile, fertile women, blessed bread and honey.

But now Neff knew he was seeing Allred for what he was, a man who had been dwelling on eternity for so long, he could not feel his feet on the ground.

"Just what are you asking me to do, Neff?"

Neff took a drink of coffee and set his cup on the table.

"Well, scale back, for starters," he said, as if the answer were plain as day and would save them both. "Stop growing them cattle and sell off half the ones you got. The land can't take it."

Allred slid back his chair and stood up. He was a bit crooked and leaned to one side, but he was still a tall man. That spring he had turned 68, but his hands looked one hundred. Now that he was standing, the blood dropped into them and they were shaking like leaves on a tree.

"I didn't come here to be told how to run my outfit," he said, and then he turned and walked out without closing the door behind him. Neff called him back, but there wasn't any coming back from the words that were said.

Out on the road, Preston had seen Allred hesitate and he asked Neff what it was about and Neff said, "I'll tell you sometime," and they rode on.

"How was it over there today?" Neff asked a short while later.

"It's going alright, I guess. We got the walls up and the roof on. Keeps the weather off us."

"I hear that," Neff said. Then he looked at the boy: "How about you, buddy boy? Old Preston isn't working you too hard, is he?"

"No sir, he ain't." The boy turned his face away from Neff and rested it against Preston's back. The two men looked at each other and Neff nodded toward the boy. Preston pointed ahead to indicate that it could wait, and they rode the rest of the way in silence.

The horses looked ahead and watched each other the way horses will. That time of year the sun fades and whitens and men and horses both glanced at it more than once as it slipped behind the mountain.

When they rode into the yard, it was twilight, and smoke rose from Neff's and Preston's cabins. "Thank you, Sara," Neff said. Jasper climbed down and opened the barn door, and Preston and Neff dismounted and walked the horses inside.

"I think I still have some jam and biscuits if you're interested. Or we could put on some water and make some honey tea. Either of those sound good to you?" Neff asked.

The boy nodded yes.

"Why don't you head on up and get it started and I'll be

along once I get the horses squared away."

The boy looked at Preston.

"Go ahead," he said. "I'll see you later."

The boy walked up to Neff's place and the two men looked after him.

"What happened over there today?" Neff asked.

Preston was in the next stall brushing Red.

"Oh, Rance said something to him."

"He didn't say what?"

"Not with words."

"What are you going to do?" Neff walked around and was checking the horse's shoes.

"Keep the boy home. Winter's coming. He doesn't need to be out in that anyway."

"Problem solved," Neff said. He loaded his pipe, smoked, and offered it to Preston.

"Well, not quite: Rance has eyes for Sara."

"Does he now?"

Preston closed the stall and sat down. "It seems that way." Neff grinned.

"Well, I guess you're just going have to bite the bullet and ask her to marry you."

"You think that will do it?"

"Maybe not, but it's a damn good start."

She knew what he was trying say. Tempted though she was to say it for him, Sara knew the words were his and to speak them with her own mouth would be to change their meaning and their meaning is what she needed to be sure of. So she waited, and as Preston fumbled his words, she watched his mouth and she noticed his tongue and how it would touch his teeth when he spoke, and she saw the wind-blown and sunny redness of his cheeks and she followed the hard line of his jaw down to his open shirt and to the soft wild hair that grew on his chest and inside that chest, his loving heart that she saw beating there.

She had spent her life traveling with her family, and as a nomad she had never been with boys or men. Nor had she had much interest in them. But now that she had stopped moving, she could imagine staying here and she did not see herself staying here alone, both for her sake and for Jasper's. Her mother, Mary, had once told her that love doesn't exist for long in any one form, and as it sheds its skins, so too must a woman's conception of it change lest she be bound to a shallow rooted and starving desire.

Mary's mother, Lou, said her own father died when she was just a girl and they buried him deep in the ground, but you'd never know he was a goner. Her mother set his place at the table, poured him a glass of fresh milk, and then she sat on the porch swing and talked to him late into the night, and when the crickets had all but petered into nothing she would climb the stairs and lay out his clothes for the next day, which is what she did for him in life.

Mary shook her head in disbelief, and then to Sara she said, "When the time comes, promise me you'll choose carefully. When you marry a man, you get the whole basket: the flesh, the blood, and the bones. The dreams. Whatever he makes and destroys. That's yours. And when he dies before you — and they usually do — you might get his ghost. It's like a bag he forgets at the train station." Mary looked at Sara and saw her puzzlement. "Having a ghost around is not so bad. He's there, as company, but he doesn't make messes."

A smile spread across Sara's face.

"Of course, he doesn't do anything else, either," Mary said and winked. "Promise me now."

"I promise, Mama."

By early spring, the horses and the deer had beaten a thin muddy path through Parley's Canyon. On a clear, sunny day, Preston rode down to Salt Lake to arrange for a judge to marry him and Sara. Herders clad in suits of wool drove their sheep west to the lower elevations. He bid them hello, and as he passed them, two massive dogs, heads like anvils, looked up at him blankly and then walked wide of him as they had learned to do with all unknown riders.

Travel was slow. It was late afternoon when he arrived in Salt Lake. He found the judge where Neff said he would and the next morning he and the judge set out for Heber Valley. The judge, a man by the name of Emory, was 30 years of age, though he looked much older. What raft of troubles must one suffer to appear so far beyond one's years? Preston turned in his saddle and saw that Emory had his eyes fixed on the ridgeline.

"See something?" Preston asked. A heavy scarf hid Emory's mouth and the acoustics of the canyon were such that when he answered, "Watching for wolves," it was as if a third man were riding with them. Preston said that he had seen wolves in the Uintas but not here, and Emory asked if Preston saw the grass under the snow. When Preston said no he did not, Emory asked if that meant it was not there. Preston turned in his saddle and the two men rode in silence.

The following afternoon, Preston and Sara married down by the river. They had thought to marry in the barn where people could find seats out of the wind, but for days they had been feeling the surging of spring and so it was settled. The first yellow warblers of the season flitted and sang in the trees along the river and the males made a fine music when they were not chasing off one another.

Joining the bride and groom were Neff, Jasper, Pickard, Pickard's wife, and their young daughter. Once the vows were exchanged, the small party feasted on a calf that had been roasting since twilight of the day before, and they drank two bottles of Pickard's whiskey and danced until their faces glistened with sweat and the sun set behind the mountains and everything darkened except the sky.

The couple exchanged gifts, and to Sara, Preston gave a beautifully tanned pair of Ute moccasins made from antelope hide and adorned with white beads.

"Now where did you find those?" she asked.

"That's for me to know," Preston said.

"Neff?" At Sara's suggestion, Neff brought out a long box and handed it to Preston.

"I think I know what this is," he said.

Sara raised her eyebrows.

"You better make sure."

"Got him a cane, did you?" Neff asked.

"You're the old wolf here, Neff," Preston laughed as he carefully unwrapped and opened the box.

"I always knew there was a devil, but now I know something about God," he said as he slipped a side-by-side double barrel shotgun from its bed of soft paper.

"Woman, I hope you know what you're doing," Neff said. "Give a man a scatter gun and he'll hunt from sun up to sun down."

"Fine by me," she said and they laughed.

Out on the road, Rance sat his horse and listened to the revelers for whom the world beyond the fire appeared as a benign black mass. But the world was still out there, harboring the deranged machinations of a man who could not rid himself of desire any more than night could rid itself of starlight.

PART FOUR

Seventeen years later.

The boys swung their lunch pails and made a game of bumping into each other as they walked to school. Ahead of them, a large yellow cat sat on the edge of the Allred field and watched it for mice. Although Allred had died some ten years before, his son Dwain still worked the cattle and like his father before him, he had enough sense to leave alone the band of trees that shaded a small spring creek where big trout spawned and an animal could get out of the sun.

The creek went under the road, and standing there the boys could see the long, shady arbor formed by the trees. The sunlight fell in there and broke the shade into alternating curtains of light and dark. In one of the dark places, the older boy, Gil, saw a man standing beneath the big tree above the swimming hole that their father Preston, Neff, and Uncle Jasper had made many summers ago by piling stones in the stream. The younger boy had already started walking again when Gil called him back.

"Come here, Cider."

"Ah, come on, Gil. We're gonna be late," Cider said, walking back begrudgingly.

"Just come here for a sec. Look in there," Gil said.

"I'm looking."

"See him, by the swimming hole?"

Cider bent down and searched.

"Yup, someone's standing there; so what?" he asked, annoyed.

"Who is that and what's he doing in there at this hour?"

"I don't know and I don't care. Now come on. Let's get to school." Cider pulled at his brother's sleeve.

"Alright," Gil said. "But he's looking right at us." Gil waved at the man and the man appeared to turn his head a little, but he did not wave back.

That afternoon on their way home from school, Gil and Cider stopped at the creek and saw that the man was still standing there.

"Tell me that ain't the damnedest thing," Gil said. He put down his lunch pail and stepped off the road and on to the path that ran along the creek, which was surely as old as the creek itself.

"Where you going?" Cider asked.

"Come on."

"Ah shit, Gil."

"Watch your mouth."

"If somebody wants to stand beneath a tree all day, that's his business. And besides, Dad's waiting on us to go fishing, remember?"

"You see any bugs?" Gil asked. He had already started down the trail.

Cider looked around and toward the river.

"I guess not," he said.

"Go on and give those bushes a good shake," Gil said.

Cider did as he was told and a couple of leaves fell and a single moth flapped into the open air.

"That's what I thought," Gil said. "You don't see any birds, neither, so what's your hurry? Ain't nothing on top, so you can't throw silk gut, and that's all Pop uses anymore." Gil looked at the sky: "You've got at least another hour, maybe more. This will take ten minutes, if that. Now come on."

Cider looked down the road each way, as if looking for some excuse not to go. But the road was empty and so he went.

As they neared the man, they caught glimpses of him through the trees and when they got within earshot, Gil stopped and called to him. "Hey mister," he said, "you need any help?" The breeze picked up and the man turned toward and away from the boys and for a moment it seemed like things might turn out all right. But the man was still silent and he kept turning toward and away from the boys as if he couldn't decide whether to address them. "Wait here," Gil said, and he walked around the brush and trees that separated him from the man. That's when he heard the rope and saw his Uncle Jasper hanging an inch off the ground.

"Oh, no," Gil whispered. Jasper's lips were black and mosquitoes were exploring his hands and face in their futile search for running blood.

"Gil?" Cider called, peering through the bushes and trying to see what was happening.

"Stay put. I'm coming right now." Gil joined Cider on the trail and he nudged him in the direction of the road.

"Who is it?" the younger boy asked.

"It's Jasper." Cider stood on the tips of his toes and tried to see his uncle.

"Jasper? What did he say?"

"Not a word."

"Well why not?"

"Cause he's dead."

Once they had returned to the road, a cloud moved across the sun and a big wind came out of nowhere and ripped along the creek and tore leaves from the trees and sent them flying every which way. Later that evening when Preston and Neff cut down Jasper, they found a dark green leaf lodged in his mouth and Preston pulled it out and placed it in his shirt pocket.

After the birth of their first boy, Gil, Preston and Sara bought 50 acres just down the road from Neff's place. The property was a half mile from the river, which they could hear at night, and well off the flood plain where in the spring the sand hill cranes would glide in on massive wings to mate and their calls would trump those of frogs or end the spells of silence and fill even human hearers with a strange sense of longing.

The Fishers had owned the land before them and they had planted apple trees that drew in the deer at dawn and dusk and if the winter had been hard enough, the eldest Fisher would get on the roof, aim through the bare trees, and shoot a deer. By the time he climbed down and got to it, the deer's heart would have pumped a hot winter apple into the snow.

In the late fall, the Fishers would harvest the fruit and sell it in town and to silver miners in Park City who would use the apples to make hard cider or to sweeten their beer. But harvest was a long ways off and so too were the cooler temperatures that would assist in the preservation of the dead. Jasper had never left the trapper's cabin behind Neff's place, and it seemed only fitting that he be placed in the food cellar while his survivors figured out what should be done with him.

Sara told Preston and Neff to be careful as they lowered

her brother into the cellar and laid him atop the ice blocks caked in sawdust. However strange the request, the men heeded it without second thought because the dead will have a say. Of course no one there had discussed where any of them would be buried. Who in a state of health would labor to find such words, however simple they may be? Preparation was what they did to survive, and to prepare for one's death was anathema and too great an acknowledgment for those who do not see with far eyes, since for them the body's roaming is all.

Preston and Neff climbed out of the cellar and brushed the sawdust from their trousers. Jasper was already starting to smell, but they kept that to themselves. "I knew this was coming," Sara said. Then she turned and walked past the now empty garden and then on up to Neff's place, and Preston and Neff weren't far behind.

Gil and Cider sat on the steps of Neff's front porch and watched their mother approach. Now in her fortieth year, Sara was lean and strong, and her long, sun-streaked hair, clear eyes, and high cheekbones were complicated by her rough, work-a-day hands and the men's boots and slacks she wore unless the situation dictated otherwise. Attending to her brother's ripening body was not one of those situations.

"Hey Mama," Cider said. Sara sat between him and Gil and put her arms around her boys and her eyes got wet.

"How are you two doing?" She pulled the boys into her and they put their heads on her shoulders and Cider cried.

"Why did he do that to himself, Mama?" Sara kissed Cider's forehead and looked at Gil. He had put himself on the top of Soapstone Mountain some twenty miles away.

"I don't know, baby."

But she did know. She knew that since that morning on the river many years ago, when her brother was just a boy and had seen the slain Utes all lined up there on the bank, he had been assailed by visions of events and calamities, the likes of which scorch the mind and deprive its bearer of footholds in the world. Knowing all that had happened and what might still, perhaps suicide was the only rational thing left to do. Though she hated the thought, she was surprised he had not committed it sooner.

Life is frightening even for the most sure-footed of travelers. How must it have been for her brother, who heard birds breathing in the dark and worms sliding into their holes? And who, when he looked at the smooth, gray river stones, saw skulls? Nor could he behold the faces of familiars and strangers without also seeing whatever troubled them in the darkness that attends every life.

A life like that would have been hard to want and keep. The roads and woodland paths are paved with headstones and the world all around is graveyard. How had Grandma Lou done it for all those years? Sara wondered if anyone would be waiting for her brother. Grandma Lou? Ben and Mary? What fool didn't know that the tragedy and beauty of life are one and the same in that life lasts for such a short while and then vanishes so completely it might not have happened at all were it not for the corpse and its memorials, though they be as soluble as names written in water?

Preston and Neff took seats on the porch and the five of them sat quietly for a long time. The full flower moon rose and cast its milky light over the fields and the road home was awash with its glow. Cider had fallen asleep with his head on his mother's lap and Gil whittled a stick. Neff got up and put a hand on Sara's and Preston's shoulders.

"I'm going to bed. You know you're welcome to stay the night," he said.

Sara put her hand on Neff's hand.

"Thank you, but we better get on home."

"You sure now?" Neff asked.

Sara nodded and at that Preston helped up Cider and walked him to the wagon. He could still smell the acrid odor of Jasper's body and he hesitated before easing Cider into the wagon. Gil was still sitting on the porch and Preston whispered at him twice before he came over.

"How are you holding up?" Preston asked.

"I've been a whole lot better, I can tell you that." Gil didn't wait for his father to say anything more because there was nothing more to say and they both knew it.

"Will you spread those blankets?'

"Yes sir."

Gil spread the blankets in the back of the wagon and Preston helped Cider lie down.

"You want to ride up front with me and your Mama?"

"Nah. I'll ride with Cide. Keep him from rolling right out the back."

Preston smiled.

"Good idea."

When she saw that the wagon was loaded, Sara turned to Neff.

"You know what the last thing he said to me was? 'Full moon tomorrow night, big sister. It will be so bright, if you don't close your eyes, it will light the inside of your head.' He said the strangest things, didn't he?" Sara looked at the moon and then across the basin. Dark scraps flying through the air. Bats.

"As sure as I'm standing here," Neff said.

That night Gil dreamed his first of many dreams about Jasper, who appeared as a much younger man and wore an expression Gil had not seen in life. They were walking along the river behind the trapper's cabin and Gil recognized the feel of the night and knew that the day of Jasper's death had not yet ended. Jasper sat on a log a beaver had felled and he put his hand on the dark pulp at the tree's center and with the kindest look on his face told Gil that he, too, was done for.

Gil awoke and went to the window and looked outside. The moon was directly overhead and the land was imbued by silver light. The leafy crowns of the apple trees glowed while the orchard corridors were as dark as dark gets. Gil understood he would have to walk there and that Jasper had already gone and would not be waiting. Nor would there be anything left to follow: The wind scours the footprints and the mice devour bread crumbs and anything that would help the newly dead find their way out of life. These are facts.

Early the next morning, Preston and Sara checked on the boys before they left for Neff's place. They sat side by side in the wagon and their draft horse Hail pulled them down the road.

"Here, get this in you." Preston handed Sara a biscuit sopped in bacon grease.

"Thank you. Where's yours?"

"Already ate it."

"Want some of mine?"

"No thank you. You eat it: It's going to be a long day."

"Yes it is," she said.

A light mist rose out of the fields and the meadow larks called to each other in the early morning quiet. The birds were hunkered down a few feet away in the short grass and still they could not be seen. Sara looked for some sign that life had been changed by the death of her brother, but nothing had and life went on as before and it always would. When they pulled into

Neff's, he was sitting on the front porch drinking his coffee.

"Seems like you were just here," he said.

"Outworn our welcome, have we?"

"You know better than that," Neff said.

"Yes I do," Preston grinned and set the wagon brake and climbed down from his seat. He offered Sara his hand, but she steadied herself using the wagon instead.

"Morning, Neff," she said.

"Hey sweet girl. You sleep alright?"

"I might have snatched an hour or two."

"That old moon keep you up did it?"

"It gave me light to think by."

"Did you figure out some things?" Neff looked serious.

"I think so," she said. "But I need your help."

Over the years, Neff had permitted the burial on his property of several Negroes, atheists, non-Christians, and Chinese immigrants who were denied burial at the local cemetery. On what basis, Neff could not say, but he figured if the townspeople could be stained in death, then greater still must have been their worries in life. To take some of the hardness out of life, Neff allowed the family of the deceased to repay him however and whenever they could, and when no family was present or when a body was laid at the edge of his property, he forgave all debt on the off chance the universe was taking measure of each person. The known bodies came on horseback or in wagons and one came in a wheel barrow and their drivers had heard of Neff's kindness, but none assumed it was so far reaching that they did not need to bring their own shovels.

Sara had spent the night piecing together all that her brother had said over the years about death, both in private and in public, and she knew that his words had gotten around and that the local cemetery wouldn't hear of his burial. Which was fine because Jasper was repulsed by the litter of caskets and by how they hid away the body and impeded its reunion with the Earth. "Just leave me in whatever clothes I'm wearing and wrap me in a blanket so I don't scare the boys," he had said once. Sara shook her head and spoke for him and for herself and for them all: "I'm here and you see me and while I'm young and strong it must seem like I will never die, but I'll be dead and gone before you know it."

Preston and Neff each took an end and they had the grave dug in short order. Sara waited for the boys at Neff's place and when they appeared the three of them walked out to the grave. Neff's and Preston's shovels stuck out of the earthworks like giant antennae. Preston walked around to where Sara and the boys were standing and he put his arm around her waist.

"Are you ready?"

"Yes."

"Okay." Preston looked at Neff and the two readied the ropes and then lowered Jasper's body into the grave. When it was done, they stood there. They were all cried out. The sun was getting hot.

"Should we say goodbye now?" Preston asked.

Sara looked at him as if he had awakened her and then she looked back into to dark hole that cooled her eyes.

"Goodbye, Jasper."

"Bye Uncle Jasper," Cider said. And then he, Sara, and Gil started for the house.

"Gil," Preston called.

"Yes sir?"

"Aren't you going to say goodbye to your uncle?"

Gil wanted to say No sir, I am not but he caught himself and said, "I already did."

———∞∞∞———

The days following the burial were long and filled with wounded silence. Jasper's death had not changed the world, but it had changed all those who had witnessed it. For who can see life end and not be further bound to the Earth? The world doesn't change, but the eyes do, the way they see the world, and when Sara awoke late in the morning, the day's stark beauty took her breath away.

She began taking long walks through the countryside in the early morning dark and saw how the living world all around forced its way out of the black dirt, the egg, and the womb to spread its kinds across the land and wherever they might take hold. She would visit her brother's grave and by the way the grasses crept she knew it was only a matter of time before the field would reclaim the bare soil that signaled Jasper's whereabouts. Neff had offered to cut a nice stone to mark the spot, but Sara asked why when the stone would just wear away in the wind and the rain and to her question Neff did not have an answer. "I can find him without it if I need to," she had said, finally.

When she would return to the house, she checked on the boys asleep in their room and then made Preston his breakfast, which she placed before him. Then she poured herself some coffee and sat down across from him at the table.

"Thank you," he said. He put his hand on hers and it was like touching bone.

"You're welcome."

"How was your walk?" Preston took a bite of egg and chewed.

"It was a walk," Sara said.

Preston looked at his plate and then at her. "Did you

see that little fox and her pups?"

"Not for a while."

Preston carried his plate to the counter and looked out the window. The sun was just coming up and he could see the slanted fence posts and the dark silhouettes of cows on their knees munching the short grass.

"Well, I hope they're alright," he said.

"I guess I don't see that it makes much difference." Sara pushed her coffee cup to the center of the table.

"There used to be a time when you did," Preston said.

Later that morning, Preston rode into town to speak with Pickard and he saw his horse tied outside the barber shop. Pickard sat in the barber's chair and behind him the barber pulled the razor up and down the strop. Preston ran his hand over his jaw and neck and the rough stubble and then he went inside.

Pickard's eyes were closed but he opened them once he heard the door close.

"Howdy, Preston."

Preston looked at each man.

"Pickard. Hey, Guy."

Guy was covering Pickard's face in warm, sweet smelling lather and he raised his eyebrows in recognition.

"Why don't you sit yourself down there? Get yourself a shave," Pickard said.

"I do need one, but I got to get back. The boys are waiting on me to go fishing."

Pickard closed his eyes again. "I'm sorry about Jasper. He was good man," he said.

Preston sat on the bench across from Pickard and put his hat beside him.

"Me too," he said.

"How are Sara and the boys holding up?"

Guy had since begun to shave Pickard's face and the razor made a crisp scrapping sound as it drove the cream out in front of it.

"Depends on the day, I guess."

"I imagine it would." Pickard folded his hands across his stomach. "What's on your mind?"

Preston asked if he could work half-days Friday until he could be sure Sara was alright, and that wasn't the kind of request a decent man could deny and so Pickard agreed. Pickard was sure Rance would be happy as a pig in mud to make up the difference and earn overtime and he joked that Preston would owe him one.

"If that were the case, I just as soon sell my soul. Make it worth my while."

"Come on now," Pickard said.

A large fly beat against the window.

"I'm just saying," Preston said.

Pickard closed his eyes as Guy did the close work under his nose.

"I'll see you Monday."

When Preston rode into the yard, the boys were sitting on the porch with all the gear.

"Good morning to you," he said.

"Good morning," the boys said.

Preston stood the horse and asked if the boys had had their breakfast and they answered "Yes sir, we did," and Preston nodded and turned the horse toward the barn.

"You boys decide where you want to fish?"

Cider looked at Gil and then at Preston and his whole face squinted in the morning sun.

"We were thinking the meadow stretch."

Preston smiled. "I can't imagine why."

Gil had gathered his share of the gear and stepped off the porch.

"It is a bona fide mystery," he said, messing Cider's hair.

Cider pushed away his brother's hand.

"Boy, you two just won't let it rest, will you?"

"Remind me, how many chances you've had so far?" Gil asked.

Preston had reached the barn and dismounted.

"If I'm not mistaken, that number would be seven," he said.

"Umm hmmm, that's what I figured. Lucky seven."

"Today will be six, thank you," the younger boy said.

Cider was getting riled so Preston put a stop to it by reminding him that if there were a book of the-worst-things-that-could-happen-to-a-boy, getting schooled by the same big trout five times running would be on page 10,000 at least.

Gil nodded. "At least. Very back of the book."

Preston knew Gil was just funning, but brothers have fought over lesser missteps so he shot Gil the look that meant he's had enough, quit it.

They took the path that led across their property and down to the spring fed creek where Jasper had hung himself days before. To the north they could see a billowing plume of black smoke rising from Allred's land. Were they newcomers to the valley they might have commented on the greasy rankness in the air, but the Allreds had been burning offal and winter kill on their spring rubbish heaps for as long as they could remember. Why this should be the year that Preston would stop and watch the fire and then say to his boys, "Look at how much smoke a single man can make," was anyone's guess, but the boys heard the words and made of them what they could.

The shadows of nimbus clouds drifted over the hills and red-winged blackbirds sang from the tops of the trees and puffed up their scarlet shoulders. Groups of them would fly together and for that moment would appear as a much larger animal that would dissipate and then rejoin a moment later.

The boys stood by as Preston reached into his bag and took out three silk gut leaders and gave one to each boy. Preston knelt on one knee and watched the creek slide past and he saw how the long blades of meadow grass cut silver furrows in the water. Large black ants walked the blades, and the ant Preston was watching fell into the water when the breeze swept through the grass.

"You ready, Pop?" Gil asked.

Preston turned around and Gil handed him his rod, which he had already rigged with line. Preston looked at the rod thoughtfully.

"Remember when you were about ten and we hiked to that lake there east of Soapstone Mountain?" he asked.

"I remember doing a lot of fishing and no catching," Gil admitted.

"I remember carrying all your gear and even you at one point. Now you're doing for me." Preston smiled at Gil and Gil got shy.

"Boy, those were some nice fish," Preston said to himself.

"Where was I?" Cider turned his hat and looked at the flies he had seated there.

"I think you were sick for that one," Preston said.

"Wouldn't you know it," Cider said.

"We'll go again."

"There?"

"Nothing's keeping us from it, I don't think. If not there, someplace else."

"There are more places to fish then there are days to fish them, ain't that right, Pop?" Gil wanted to know.

"That is the truth," Preston said.

"You going to work ants today, then?" Gil asked, watching his father poke through a paper fold of flies.

"As is my habit, I reckon." Preston attached the now-dampened gut leader to the line and to the tip of that he added a furry black ant tied with thread and twine fray. "What about you?"

Gil scratched his scant beard. "Sun's getting up there. I'll probably fish deep. What do you think, Cider? You think I'm wrong?"

Cider looked up and down the creek.

"I guess we're fixing to see." Cider looked from his brother to the sky and then to the water. "I'm going to walk for a bit and see what all is going on."

"That's a fine idea if there ever was one, little brother."

The old trees creaked in the wind like someone trying at a violin. Later, as they walked the banks, the boys snatched the slow-moving locust nymphs from where they sat in the plants, eating leaves and warming in the sun, the descendents of the great swarms that came in times of drought, blotted out the sun, and fell like snow upon the doomed fields of wheat and barley. The boys looked for the deep pools and the slow, dark bars of water along the banks and into those they threw the writhing hoppers.

Stunned by the cold, the nymphs kicked once or twice and then stilled. Sometimes they would collide with debris and climb on, or the current would deliver them to the bank opposite the boys, but most times the nymphs would remain within range of taking and from out of the black-green deeps the domed heads of big trout would swim up and the boys would freeze at the sight and they would not move until the trout snapped the hopper from the water and then returned to a world that human eyes would never see.

This went on until Preston and the boys came to a place where the creek bent and the water went slack at the elbow. No cattle had trod there and thus the meadow grass was thick with shade and alive with insects. Certain a trout would be there waiting for some hapless bug, Preston laid his ant right in the crook of the elbow. The ant sank and Preston drew it back and dressed it with a light film of bacon grease. Then he flicked the ant into the grass and watched it tumble and drop atop the water.

"Damn, that ant looks good," Gil said. "I'm waiting for it to start crawling up your line." The ant hadn't floated six inches when a trout came off the bank and slammed it with a splash. The line went taut and cut a small "v" in the water as the trout pulled down and away.

"He's fighting for his life, ain't he Pop?"

"He is at that." Preston gradually lifted the rod tip and as he did so the trout caught the light and flashed like a mirror under the water. When the fish was within reach, he lifted its chin, clutched it by the throat, and held it in the air.

"Pretty fish," he said.

"Should we call it good, then?" Gil asked, grinning.

Cider just shook his head. "I tell you what, if you're trying to get my goat, you did it."

"Ah, c'mon Cide," Gil said. Cider ran the silk gut through his hand and straightened it. When Cider didn't respond, Gil knew he should let it go, but he couldn't.

"These last few days have been real tough; I was just funning."

"Yeah, well, I'm just not there yet." Cider then turned and

headed for the big trout that had eluded him all spring.

"Give him time," Preston said.

"I know. I just wish he'd hurry and get back to his old self." Gil snapped a grass stem and stuck it in his mouth. Dozens of barn swallows had suddenly filled the air to feed on unseen insects. Somewhere beyond the trees the dull, pounding sound of running horses.

"Are you back to your old self, then?" Preston asked, placing his hand on Gil's back. Gil watched his brother disappear around the bend.

"No sir, and I don't think I ever will be."

When Cider reached the big trout's home he sat down in a patch of hound's tongue and watched the water. Rafts of foam, seeds, grass bits, and flower petals floated by, and a golden crane fly hovered above the film and dipped the tip of its abdomen in the water. Here the bank was a good four feet high and dark with rain and a fresh chunk of ground had recently fallen into the creek.

The breeze shifted and brought the sour stench of skin and guts roasting in the sun. Cider spread the curtain of high blades where the flies were swarming and he saw the mangled heap of hide and feet and strewn about were the fly and ant slathered entrails and untouched stomach of the devoured. "Poor bastard, you got outsmarted, didn't you?" Cider moved up wind and pulled a fly from his hat. He looked at it from all angles and finding some defect he plucked its twine fray body until it was double its size.

That done, he ran his hand through his hair until his finger tips shined with oil, which he then applied to the underside of the fly and its hackle. Weeks ago, Cider and Preston had gone hunting for pheasant in the stiff yellow grasslands below the foothills, and Preston had shot a rooster that came down in a shower of feathers. Cider saw how they rocked and shined as they fell and he noted the flexible quill and put a few of them in his coat pocket. At home that night he wrapped the shank of the hook with the feather and he felt the weight of every fish he had ever lost lifted and knew his odds were going to change.

The fly he held presently was fourth generation and once he had oiled it and preened the hackle, he tied it on with a clinch knot and then returned to studying the water. He looked up the creek and watched it come. In his mind he saw Jasper hanging and turning toward him in the shadows, and then his mother's hard look and Jasper's body laying wrapped in the grave like some giant larvae. Then the sounds of leaping water.

Cider could not see the big trout, but he knew what he heard. He held four coils of line in his hand and cast just once. The fly settled in but it did not sink as it floated toward the place where Cider thought the trout was holding.

The big trout held in three feet of water. Above him floated rafts of scum and vegetation and all manner of seeds and their husks and once in a while a burr or a clump of deer hair or better yet the golden crane flies or drakes hovering an inch above the film. In his fish brain he might have known he could take them with some effort, but why do that when the plump nymphs of a dozen species practically drifted into his mouth?

That might have been the trout's thinking, but then Cider's ample fly came riding atop the water. The supple thorax and abdomen and the tiny legs dangled just below the surface. With the twitch of his fins the trout rose and sucked the whole fly into his mouth and did he feel the delicate sweep of wings on the bed of his tongue and then the ache of steel on his teeth? The hook drove a hair shy of the old trout's olfactory lobe and what choice was there now except to jump into the bright killing air and have a look?

"Sweet hell!" Cider yelled as the trout jumped and arced above the water. He raised his rod high above his head and kept the line tight as the trout launched into the air once, twice, three times before milking gravity and dropping heavy as a stone in the deep water. "Alright," Cider said. Judging by the angle of the line, the trout was directly below him, and fearing it might see him, bolt, and snap him off, Cider took two steps back and waited. Nor would he let the trout drift back any farther lest he wrap himself in the branches of a cottonwood tree a beaver had felled last summer. That is what his time with the trout had taught him to do.

Clouds were drifting up from the southwest and where he stood was lighted by sun, but everything down from him was covered in cloud shadow. The creek stretched away darkly and balls of gnats revolved above it like intricate machines and at his feet small black spiders raced through the dead grass and over his boots as if he were not there and Cider wondered at all that went on beneath the water and what else did he not see and why should the dead be the only ones to know anything for sure? The big trout hunted the flies and he hunted the trout, but what exactly is it that is hunting him besides hunger, time, and bad dreams?

The trout slipped back and Cider said "I thought you might do that" as he lifted the rod to see if the trout would rise. The trout did rise and Cider saw him clearly for the first time and he was round as a stove pipe and two feet long. His lower jaw jutted out and Cider could see a couple rusty hooks hanging there and he was sure they were his. In a rush, the trout surged forward and out into the current, his shoulders swaying side-to-side as he gained momentum. "Hold on now."

Cider eased the rod tip up and he could feel the trout weaken until finally he gave in to the force of the line and the will of the boy who held it.

Cider walked into the water and guided the trout between his boots. "Remember me? I've been hunting you." A small garter snake had coiled in grass that hung over the water and it tasted the air as Cider put his rod under his arm and bent to the trout. Cider didn't know what he was going to do until the moment he put his hand under the trout's soft, cold belly and felt his buoyant heft. He saw his silky blue fins wafting and the shining eyes that looked at him the same way they looked at everything and he popped the hook from the trout's jaw. "You owe me," Cider said. The trout rested for a few moments and then thrust its tail fin and disappeared into the dark water.

Cider found Preston and Gil sitting beneath the cottonwoods and the ground there was white with seed.

"Pull up a seed," Preston joked, patting the ground beside him.

Cider leaned his rod against the backside of the tree with the others there and then took a seat beside his father.

"How did it go?" Gil asked, handing his brother the canteen of water.

"Well, let's just say I knocked and no one answered."

"Next time," Preston said.

"Yep, next time."

"That's all right; we got plenty," Gil said. "This is a great little stretch of crooked water, isn't it?"

"Yes it is," Cider said.

"Jasper showed it to you, didn't he?"

Cider nodded.

"Yes," he said, "and Neff showed it to him."

Gil leaned back and put his hat over his face. "Do we know who showed it to Neff?"

"Another bona fide mystery?" Cider smirked.

Gil pushed up his hat with his finger. "The world is done chalk full of them, apparently."

"Maybe so," Cider said, turning serious. "Or maybe we just don't understand what's right in front of our face."

"What's eating you?" Preston asked.

Cider shook his head but he couldn't say anything and his body shook with whatever he was holding inside.

"It's alright." Preston put his hand on Cider's shoulder.

"Up until now, life's made pretty good sense," Cider said as he thumbed away the water and dirt from his face. "Most days I get up with the sun and most days I go down with it; the deer come down in the winter and go up in the summer; and I know if I put a seed in the ground and keep it wet, it'll grow and that a tight fence will keep the rabbits from it; and all the grimness: I understand that. It doesn't always make me feel so good knowing it, but that isn't the same as not making sense."

"Fifteen years ain't a whole lot of time to figure out something as big as life," Preston said.

"Maybe in another 15 years I'll understand why Jasper did what he did? I haven't seen a thing that can explain it. It doesn't figure, Pop. Not one bit."

Preston took the canteen from Cider, drank, and then handed it back to Gil.

"Maybe not," Preston said.

"Meaning what?" Gil asked.

"Well, meaning that you can't really understand what life means for someone like Jasper. What he actually saw of the world and what he claimed to have seen weren't always easy to separate. It's hard to know much of anything about a person like that." Preston paused here and squinted at the sun. "It's hard to say what's true about him. And if you can't know the truth about someone, where does that leave you? That's the question your Mama and I have been asking since the day we rode into this valley. I guess we got our answer."

The wind gusted and blew grit and they pulled down their hats and waited for it to pass. Not two feet from Preston's boots a gopher snake had lain still and when the wind picked up it slid off and the tall grass shuddered and not a soul there was the wiser. Preston leaned back on one arm and looked at his boys.

"When Jasper was about 11 years old we had one of those big winters you don't see but every 10 years or so. We were still living in the trapper's cabin and the snow was so high, we could just see the top of Neff's roof from our front door. It was something, I'll tell you. I hadn't seen anything like it and Neff hadn't seen it but three times in his life."

A western tanager flew into view, and before vanishing into the greenery along the creek, its bright yellow breast and fiery face ignited the air. Once it was gone, Preston continued. "Yes, that was one hell of a winter. The snow was all the way up to the windows and some nights the roof would start creaking and we were sure the damn thing was going to cave on us. I don't know how many times I got up there to clear the snow. By the time I was done, the snow was a good four foot up the side of the cabin so you could just see the tops of the windows."

"Old Neff have to dig you out?" Cider asked.

"You'd think, but no. Between your mother and me, we kept the door clear," Preston said. "One night it was snowing and your mother and I were in our room getting ready to turn in and in comes Jasper saying there's a black wolf staring down at him through the window."

Gil guffawed.

"That's what he said. We'd heard wolves, and I might have caught a glimpse of one in the mountains, and certainly we'd heard them rumored, but Neff was the only one to have seen them in valley."

"When was that?" Cider asked.

"I think he said he was fifteen years old when that happened. But there was Jasper, his face flushed like something awful, saying a wolf was right outside his window. I could see he was upset, but then my life up to that point hadn't involved seeing any wolves in the valley, in which case he's telling me one thing and my whole life is telling me another. So I asked him if he dreamed it. You know what he says to me?"

"What?" both boys asked at the same time.

"He said 'I did if I am dreaming you now.'" At this Preston made a funny grimace and the boys chuckled. "So I pull on my pants and boots, grab the Colt and I head outside. Mind you that from the time Jasper came into the room until the moment I was standing outside, not two minutes had passed. The snow was falling big and slow and the fields beyond the cabin were blue-white and the night was so dark that the fields seemed to glow. I couldn't remember ever seeing so well at night," Preston said, all nostalgic.

"Did you see the wolf then?" Cider cut to the chase.

"So I got the Colt out in front of me and I turn the corner expecting to see the-lord-only-knows-what and there, laying in the snow, is the hind leg of an elk. The whole damn thing. I put my hand on it and I kid you not, it was still warm."

"Come one now," Gil said.

"I swear on my life."

"You swear on Mama's and Cider's?"

"I do. Anyone else?"

"No sir," Gil said, embarrassed.

"Alright then. Trailing off across the hard pack I see wolf tracks, big as flap jacks." Preston joined his thumbs and middle fingers to show the size of the tracks.

"You sure they were wolf? Dwain has that shepherd," Cider said.

"Yes, I'm sure: These tracks were twice the size of any dog. There was no light to speak of and they were still big and deep enough to cast shadows. I followed them as long as I could and then I looked out ahead, maybe three hundred yards, a little more, and sure enough, there was the wolf, big and black as charcoal, outlined against the cemetery hill. How he got from Jasper's window to that hill in two minutes is for someone smarter than me to say."

Swallows were again on the move and a big trout rose and took two drakes from surface in quick succession. Then it rose again.

"One of you boys get after it," Preston said.

"Go ahead, Cide," Gil said, giving his brother a little nudge with his boot.

"You go on."

"Nah, I'm liking this shade too much," Gil said and then addressed his father. "Stranger things have happened, though, haven't they Pop?"

"Has a wolf ever brought you a piece of perfectly good elk meat in the dead of night?" Preston asked, incredulous.

"It just so happens," Gil grinned.

"I didn't think so," Preston said. "Besides," he continued, "that ain't the least of it. A couple weeks later, evening rolls around and Jasper says he's going to snow shoe out in the meadow. That boy was always doing something. Always out-and-about looking for critters and what not. I asked him if

Sara knew about it and he said she did. 'And she's okay with it?' He said she was, so I said 'Okay, well, get to it.' I reminded him he had about two hours before dark and off he went. Well, two hours pass and still no Jasper. It was damn near full dark when Sara sat down to put on her boots. I says to her, 'Where do you think you're going?' and she looks up at me and says, 'Where do you think I'm going?' I insisted she let me go get him and she said, 'no,' and then I said, 'Well, at least let me go with you,' and she said, 'Ain't necessary. Set the table, please.' And she stuffed the Colt in her belt and went out."

Cider started rummaging through Preston's bag. "You bring anything to eat, Pop?"

"There's some of Neff's jerky in there. The bread is wrapped in that cloth. Honey's in the jar."

"I want some. Hand me a cut of that jerky, will you Cide?" Gil asked.

Preston waited for the boys to get their food before continuing.

"I had sat there long enough and just as I'm putting on my boots to head out after them, in they come. Jasper looked a little tired was all, but then I looked at your mother and I could tell something had happened. I asked her if everything was okay and she shifted her eyes to Jasper and said, 'yes,' and I knew that meant 'no.' I've lived with your Mama long enough to know when to talk and when to not so we sat down to dinner and I don't think two words got spoken.

"After we ate, Jasper headed off to bed and we cleaned up and turned in as well. It wasn't until after Jasper had left for school the next morning that she told me. As I understand it, your Mama had just reached the meadow fence when she sees Jasper shoeing toward her. She said he apologized up and down and said he would have been home earlier, but that he couldn't because he had to hide."

"The wolf come back?" Cider asked, and the second he did so he realized there wasn't no hiding from a wolf and so on the tail of that question he asked another. "Hide from what?"

"Well, Jasper said he was walking below the hills when he saw eyes watching him from the ridgeline."

"How many?" Cider asked, licking his lips.

"I don't know. A bunch, so he high-tailed it to some brush and hid out. Jasper was a smart kid. It didn't take him long to realize that he'd be in for it should whatever was watching him decide to come down off that ridge, so he made a break for it."

"Oh boy, I'll bet he ran like hell. I know I would," Cider said.

"Yeah, well, he told your Mama he hadn't gotten far when he heard a horse coming up behind him. When he saw a man on the horse, he thought maybe it was someone he knew, hell he hoped it was, so he stopped and waited for the rider. Right away he could see the rider was a Ute."

"A real life wagon burner?" Gil leaned toward his father.

"I don't much care for that talk. We would do whatever we had to were someone threatening to take our land, which, truth be told, they lived on better than us white folks ever could," Preston said.

Gil nodded that he understood.

"Who was the man, then?" Cider asked.

"Hard to say. Jasper said he came to within twenty feet and then stopped, and when Jasper would walk, he would follow at a distance. I guess this went on all the way to the meadow fence, but when Jasper turned to point him out to your mother, he was gone. Your Mama walked out into the meadow to see if she could find some tracks; she found not a one."

Preston paused here to watch a large yellow bellied marmot patrol its territory across the creek, its short fluffy tail flopping from side-to-side in a display sexual swagger.

"He's real tough, ain't he?" Gil said. Then he aimed his imaginary rifle and fired: "Boom." At the noise, the marmot rose on its hind legs and made a high pitched chirp. Then another. "That's right, whistle pig. I could have had you." The marmot then scurried into its burrow.

"Like just about every other critter, they get careless during the breeding season," Preston said.

"You ever eat one of those, Pop?"

"Can't say that I have. I ate a porcupine, though."

"How was it?"

"Good, surprisingly. Boy, my pa could cook meat, any meat," Preston said as if he had a mouthful of his father's grub. "Us kids could always tell if my ma had cooked it because it never turned out as well. But we ate everything she put in front of us."

"Hey Pop?" Gil asked.

"Yeah."

"Is that the sort of thing that gets passed on?"

"Knowing how to cook meat?" Preston asked.

"No, what Jasper had."

"Bad luck?"

"I guess."

"I wouldn't know, but I hope not." Preston looked hard at Cider and then at Gil. "Why would you ask such a thing?"

Gil stood up and brushed off his pants.

"Well, I reckon so I know what to look for."

—⟨∞⟩—

A month had passed since Jasper's burial and a month since they had sat together as a family, although it felt much longer judging by how hard it was to meet each other's eyes. Sara pushed the biscuits toward her boys and they each took one and spread jam on it and then ate.

"I need one of you to come into town with me today," Sara said. Gil pointed at Cider and Cider pointed at Gil, and with mouths full of biscuit, they both said "He'll go." Sara and Preston looked at each other and smiled for the first time in weeks. They were surprised by the other's face; it had been that long since they had really looked at each other.

"Which one of you has got nothing going on today?" Preston asked.

Cider chased his biscuit with a gulp of coffee.

"We're going hunting, right Pop?" he said.

"Well," Preston started.

"I'm going to. . ." Gil struggled here. "I got something I got to do. I just don't remember what."

"What do you think, Sara? Should we let Lady Luck decide?" Preston asked.

"I think yes," she said.

Preston got up and took a mug from the fireplace mantle and dumped a small coin into his palm.

"Ah, Pop. Gil always wins."

"Are you ready?" Preston laid the coin on top of his thumb nail.

"You can call it, little brother."

"Don't matter who calls it: I'll still lose."

"*Doesn't* matter," Preston said.

"Yes sir," Gil said.

"Call it." Preston flipped the coin.

When they got to town, Sara sat the horses and Gil hopped out of the wagon and tied them to the post. She tore her list in two and gave him half. He read the list.

"When you're finished getting those things, bring the wagon around back and we'll load the lumber."

"Yes ma'am."

When the two entered the store, Rance was standing at the counter talking with the clerk.

"Good morning Mrs. Wood, Gil," the clerk said as he placed a few items in Rance's dry goods box. A bottle of hell's blood whiskey towered above the goods and Rance snatched it up and slid it into the box. Then he nodded in their general direction.

"Good morning, Mr. Barlow," Sara said.

Gil nodded at Mr. Barlow and looked warily at Rance, who wore a heavy red beard and held a pipe in the corner of his mouth. When he noticed Gil looking at him, he took out the pipe.

"You got something on your mind, youngster?"

"I got lots on my mind, though I don't see how that's any concern of yours."

"Gil," Sara said, taking him aside.

"That's all right, Mrs. Wood. I asked him a question and he answered." Rance grinned at Gil. "Put a boy on horseback and there's no telling where he'll ride, ain't that right Mr. Barlow?"

"I suppose it is," Mr. Barlow said, looking from person to person and smiling nervously. "That will be 50 cents."

Rance dug into his pocket and laid the coins on the counter. "Give my regards to your husband," Rance said, and then he picked up his box and walked out.

Gil loaded their supplies and then drove the wagon around back. Sara was already there with Mr. Barlow's son, Ed, with whom she discussed the details of the lumber. Another man worked the big saw and the noise was entire. When Sara saw Gil, she pointed to a stack of boards, held up both hands, and mouthed the word "ten." Gil nodded and slipped on his gloves. As he neared the stack, he could smell the new boards and it helped him forget the task of pulling them. He had loaded two when he noticed an old crate lined with burlap. He took off his gloves and knelt down.

Inside the crate were two dogs and they couldn't have been more than two months old. He picked up each one in turn and felt their soft coats and loose puppy skin. They licked his face and he smelled their clean, sweet breath. In the meantime Sara had come and knelt beside him.

"What do we have here?" she asked, scooping up one of the puppies. "Where's your mama?" Sara looked into the dog's black eyes. Then she looked at Gil.

"Have you seen her?"

"No ma'am."

"You best find her."

"Why?"

"Well, if you were about to leave home, wouldn't you want a chance to say 'goodbye' to me?"

"They're mine? Both of them?" Gil asked.

"Well, let's see what Mr. Barlow wants for them." Sara could see Mr. Barlow through the back windows and when he looked at her she pointed to the dogs and he came out.

"Did you get your wood alright," he asked, looking at the wagon.

"We're working on it," she said. "These your dogs?"

"Yes they are."

"How much you asking for them?" Gil asked, squinting up at Mr. Barlow.

"What are they worth to you?"

"That ain't the same thing, is it?"

"Give the man a price," Sara said.

"I got a dime is all."

"A nickel a piece then?"

"If you'll take it," Gil said.

Mr. Barlow looked around and, not seeing what he was looking for, he lifted up the crate.

"What do we have here?" he asked, and from under the crate he pulled a muddy sign that said Free Dogs. "Keep your dime, son. You're doing me a favor."

⁕

Preston and Cider stood on the ridge and listened for grouse in the valley below them. The wind was coming from the south and it was loud across their ears.

"I can't hear a thing, Pop, can you?"

"Put on your dog ears," Preston said, whispering and cupping his ear with the hand that did not hold the shotgun.

Cider held his hands just so and turned his head to test his new ears.

"There you go; works well, doesn't it?"

"Yes sir. Now all I need is a dog nose and we'd be set." Cider scrunched his nose and looked at Preston.

"Well, if you find one, let me know."

Half the valley lay in shadow and a pair of chickadees flitted and chattered in the sagebrush. There had been no rain but still the air smelled wet and clean and the toes of Preston's and Cider's boots were dark from kicking dew. Once the chickadees had moved on, the two returned to listening for the peculiar, high plop call of the sage grouse. They were in no hurry. Preston dug a biscuit he had slathered in jam and handed it to Cider, who carefully unwrapped it and offered half to Preston.

"You go ahead. I've got another in here," he said, patting his jacket pocket. The two sat for a long time, downwind, and eventually the world they knew was there but seldom saw came to them in staggered order. First, a coyote in a raggedy coat walked the ridge on the other side, alternately putting his nose to the ground for a pungent whiff of prey or spore and then up again to listen for the sounds of those who would prey upon him: The click of a trigger, a cough, a whispered killing word, or the padded steps of wolves. Preston wondered how many times some silent, low-lying animal had watched him go by and did it feel anything like he was feeling now?

Preston and Cider looked at each other and smiled, as though they were seeing something no two men had seen before or would see again. Next came a doe and her scentless fawn, which must have caught the scent of the coyote because it laid in the sage and the doe high-stepped it in the direction of the coyote and then dropped over the ridge so that should he come this way he would follow her instead. "Your Mama and I would do that for you," Preston whispered. Then a grouse called from directly across the valley and the feeling of the day changed again.

Everything in whispers now.

"Here," Preston said, offering the gun to Cider. "This is your bird."

"Yes sir." Cider carefully opened the breach, saw the cartridges, and closed it again. Preston held out his hand, palm up, and used it as a slate.

"We're here and the bird's about here," he said, pointing. "We want to drive him up and pin him against the hill."

"Yes sir," Cider said.

"Give me a chance to drop down below him. Once I get about here, I want you to walk down to the bottom here and get ready. Make sure the gun is on your shoulder. You ready?"

"Yes sir."

Preston cut twenty yards down the ridge to get well below the grouse and then he dropped into the valley. A black-tailed jackrabbit broke cover and bolted toward the grouse. "Damn it all," Preston whispered. But suddenly the jack cut right and darted up and over the ridge, its powerful hind legs jettisoning him high into clear blue sky. Preston looked up and Cider tilted his head as if to say "that was close" and Preston gestured back that it was. Then he started walking again and when he came within twenty feet of the grouse, he waited for Cider to cut down to the valley floor and put the gun to his shoulder.

Cider's hands were sweating. The big gun was pointed in the direction of the grouse and Cider had both eyes open in case the bird broke left and with his right eye he watched his father work his way toward the bird. He swore to Christ that his hands were turning into water and he wiped his trigger hand on his trousers and of course at that exact moment the grouse exploded from the sage and flew straight toward the ridgeline.

"He's up!" Preston yelled.

Cider raised the gun and fired just as the bird crested the ridge.

"You hit him!" Preston said, rushing to where Cider stood, smoke pouring out the barrel. "Why did you wait so long to shoot?"

"You don't want to know." Cider opened the breach and

pulled out the spent shell and put it in his pocket.

They weaved through the sage with their eyes on the ground. Sun-baked coyote turds made of hair, nail, and bone lay strewn along the corridor up to the ridge.

"I got blood over here," Cider said, rubbing the blood from the tip of a sagebrush and working it between fingers. "And feathers." They were long and fine and Cider slipped them into his jacket pocket.

Preston walked over and studied the brush. "Good eyes. Let's see how well you hit him." They walked side by side and ran their hands atop the sage, sometimes parting it if it became too heavy, until finally they came to the grouse, which had hidden itself away in its final moments. Cider reached down and pulled out the bird and held it up. He tilted the bird so its head rolled off its chest of soot yellow feathers. "Pretty birds, aren't they?" Preston mused. And for a moment it was beautiful and warm, but then a drizzle of blood thick as syrup ran out the bird's neck and down the front of Cider's hand.

"That was a hell of a shot," Preston said, taking the gun. "And none too soon: Any longer and he would have put the ridge between you."

"I know it." Cider rubbed his shoulder.

"Did you get kicked?"

"A little," he said.

"You rest that shoulder and a give the old fella a chance to round up a bird or two."

"Good enough," Cider said. "You want to try below the mounds?"

"I'm thinking so," Preston said, and the two of them headed down into the valley where the shade was still plentiful.

The mounds were so called because people were buried there. Several years back, the basin had another big winter and when the sun came in a hurry the rivulets of snow melt carried away the dirt and rocks and uprooted the vegetation and bones started turning up everywhere. They had thought to rebury them but Neff told them to leave them where they lay and so that is what they did. But then the animals dragged the bones away from the mounds where they could gnaw them in the open, and in their drive to eat the sparse and tender grasses that grew in the shade of sagebrush, the cattle trod and crushed the skulls that shone like dirty gold mushrooms. Though unnamed and of uncertain origin, bones scattered across the land was an unsettling sight to all who happened on them and it was not long before a fence of devil's rope three strands deep appeared below the mounds and so enclosed the dead to the extent that barbed wire could.

Cider could feel the sweat run down his spine to the crack of his ass and the bird's limp neck grow soggy in his hand. Neither he nor Preston spoke as they took careful steps below the mound, and when the breeze would come and go, Cider wondered if it took the wild and dead smell of the bird with it and what if anything did it announce to the small brained animals whose senses were so acute they could taste a man's breath in the air? Preston stopped and held up his hand. They waited. Then it came: The ripping, high popping call of the grouse.

The lay of the land spread the sound east and west and Preston wavered before pointing his hand in the direction of the call.

"He's about fifteen yards up the mound," Preston said.

Cider waited for his father to say they'd find another bird.

"Hold this." Preston gave Cider the gun.

"Where you going?"

Preston knew this was Cider's way of saying, "Don't go. We'll find more birds up ahead. We always do." But the bird was close and, bones or no bones, Preston had his mind set.

"I'm going after that bird." Preston gripped the top and middle wire between the barbs.

"Alright, well, what do you want me to do?"

"I want you to stay put. He'll break right or left." He looked up at the mound and then back at Cider. "You just hang back and watch where he drops, okay?"

"Yes, sir."

Preston spread the wires like the jaws of a trap and slipped through, easy as pie. Then he called for the gun.

"You want me to put it over or through?" Cider asked.

"Let's keep it low. Go ahead and slip it through there." Preston caught the barrel as Cider fed it through the top and middle wire and he had almost reached the breach when the grouse called again, louder and closer.

In his haste, Preston pulled the gun before the breach had cleared the wire and the forward trigger caught a barb and the gun fired, hitting him in the groin and thigh. A gun is a far cry from a stone, humanity's first weapon. It cannot be dropped or hurried. All its debts are paid in blood, and so too are its mistakes. Cider climbed over the fence and knelt by his father. He could see the blood welling between his father's fingers.

"God damn," Preston said, doing his best to stop what could not be stopped.

"I'm going to get help," Cider said, on the verge of panic. He took off his jacket and covered his father. Preston could feel the blood rushing out of him and he knew there would not be time. "Stay here with me, boy," he thought. But he could not bring himself to concede his imminent death nor destroy Cider's hope that he would live and that one day they would recollect that afternoon as wise and seasoned men.

"Alright, you go," he said, clutching Cider's hand. And Cider slipped through the wire and ran through the sage and leapt over rocks. When Cider was no longer visible, Preston laid flat on the ground and closed his eyes. He could feel all that ground holding him. He saw Sara sitting on the river's edge when she was just a girl, Jasper in her lap. She squinted in the sunlight and smiled and he shuddered at the memory and the sadness that followed it. And the boys: Gil standing waist-deep in the river, holding up his first trout in the evening light, and Cider running through the field, his feet touching the ground just long enough to leave it. Death and life chase us equally and the dark moment is when we realize the former has caught us first.

Preston opened his eyes. A fly crawled along the ground. The dirt was soaked and he could smell himself in it. His warm piss, sweat, and blood. His spirit in there somewhere, drowning.

Will I sleep the cold sleep? he wanted to know.

Will you keep me, Earth, one less wandering, dirt-bound son?

Gil and Cider peered from the kitchen window as Sara and Rance talked out in the yard. Rance's horse stood at his side and every now and then the wind would gust and drag its hair southward and up as if gravity had momentarily lost its grip on it. The dogs were out there, too, and they sniffed Rance and the horse as if they had just come from the woods.

"Watch Mama," Gil said. "If she laughs or smiles, it means that sumbitch is staying on and we're in trouble."

"Pop is surely turning in his grave at the sight of this," Cider said.

Sara did not laugh or smile, but she shook Rance's hand

when he offered it.

"Ah shit, there it is," Gil said. "Mama made a deal with the devil."

As Sara walked toward the house with the dogs in tow, Rance looked after her and then past her to the window and to Cider and Gil.

"That sumbitch is looking right at us," Cider said.

"I see that. You ain't welcome here," Gil said.

Rance nodded and put on his hat. Then he grinned, climbed on his horse, and left.

"What are you two doing standing there? Spying on me?" Sara asked.

"I always wondered what the devil looked like," Gil said. "Now I know."

"That may be true, but devil or not, he's the only one interested in helping out around here. We can't go another year without some help."

"What about Neff?" Cider asked.

"I'm not going to ask Neff to do a dang thing; he's got his own troubles without me adding mine."

"But he'd do it for you, Mama. And he'd do it for nothing."

"And that's exactly why I ain't asking him," Sara said.

Gil sat at the table and put his face in his hands.

"Why are you so upset about this, Gil?" Sara put her hands on his shoulders. "It's for a little while. After the harvest, we'll send him packing and try to get someone else."

"Oh Mama," Gil said. And he came out from behind his hands so his mother could see it was already too late.

PART FIVE

Cider stopped at the tree line and watched the house in the gray light of dawn. The smell of snow was on the wind and black midges searched for each other on the ice patches. He had not slept for two days, and he was delirious and filthy from all he had seen and done. Still spattered with his brother's blood, the empty shotgun teetered in his hand, a scale of justice by which rights and wrongs had yet to be reckoned.

The house was still and Cider knew if Rance weren't up now, he likely wouldn't wake for some time. Such is the toll of hell's blood. Rance's whiskey slumber would give Cider time to gather the tools and dig a grave for the apples. He waited and watched as the sky lightened. Dime and Slowdee were not about and they could be gone for days, roaming the valley, hills, and the lower mountains. Or perhaps they had doubled back and were now sprawled, stinking, and sleeping on Rance's bed. The three of them breathing a vapor of whiskey, plaque, and standing blood.

The yard was quiet. He had stood the tools on the corner of the house, and he went for them. Cider took long strides and he had almost made it to the corner of the house when he saw the rogue dog peering at him from the corner of the barn. Head low. Tail stiff. Ears flat. The Creator was said to have made the heavens and the Earth from nothing. And so it was that even in his wretched depletion, Cider conjured the image of the rogue standing over Gil, claiming him, and now, as then, a sickening rage welled inside him. He squeezed the shotgun. Had he believed in the soul, he would have given his for two shells with which to blow the rogue into the snow. "Stay right there, you son of a bitch. I got something for you."

Cider went to his window and lifted it. He leaned the shotgun against the wall, shucked off his boots, and climbed into his room. He listened. House sounds. Then he crossed the hall into his mother and father's room and he looked at the bed as if they might still be in it and then to the bureau for shotgun shells. Seeing none, he looked at the wall peg where the Colt had hung in its holster for as long as he could remember. It was not there. He searched in the drawers and under the bed and then he moved to the big pine trunk Preston had made his first summer in the valley.

Down the hall, Rance shifted in his bed and coughed and one of the dogs jumped to the floor and lay down against the wall. Cider knelt in front of the trunk and saw that it was locked. Then he remembered the key he had taken off his mother's neck, and he took it from his own neck and slipped it in the lock. In the deep quiet of the room, the opening lock made a big sound and set Cider's heart racing. A wave of nausea started in his stomach and rose into his mouth. He swallowed some spit to give his stomach something to do. Then he opened the trunk lid until it rested on its hinges.

The top trays held various documents, including the deed to the land and letters from Preston's sister, and stacked in the corners were coins and several small nuggets of panned gold, Preston's father's watch, and what appeared to be a small jar of Neff's medicinal buds. He lifted out the trays and placed them on the floor. Staring up at him was the topsy-turvy doll Preston had found some twenty years ago, and it was as strange now as it was then. Next to it were two flat boxes in the bottom of the chest. The Colt was there. The holster had been rubbed with saddle soap, and once the trays were lifted out, the smell wafted into the room. He took out the gun, saw it was loaded, and strapped it on.

The smaller box of the two was sleek and shiny, while the other was rough hewn from wood though not unbeautiful. Whatever sense of calm he felt at the sight disappeared when he opened the smaller box and the small silver snake writhed inside. Cider threw the box into the chest where it lay open. When the snake did not glide out, he knew he had been duped, just as his father had been years earlier. What awaited him in the larger box? He wondered. The box was covered in dust and Cider concluded it had not been opened or even touched for some time. Years, maybe. He tried the clasp and it would not budge, so he took out his knife and pried it open. Even then, the lid would not loosen until he ran the knife tip around it, cutting the grime of years that had hardened there. He slowly opened it.

A row of four figurines made of clay and blood gazed across the centuries, their animal faces those of primordial nightmares. Cider lifted one from the cloth and recognized it as one he had seen painted on Gil's wall. Before Preston was interred, Cider touched his face one last time and that was what he felt now and that emptiness traveled up his arm and with it a sickening fear that overran his body. At his feet, ants swarmed a cricket. He dropped the figurine into the box and snapped it shut.

How his mother and father had come by these noxious pieces, he would never know. Yet he did not question why they had kept them from him, since he too would now spend his life trying to forget what he had seen. He left the room as he had found it and quietly went into the kitchen where he drank some water and tried to eat a piece of old bread. In the throes of whatever had seized him he could not get it down. "God damn," he whispered.

The sun had burned off most of the clouds and the day was now bright and cut with the stench of coal smoke. The dog was long gone. Cider walked out to where he had stood and noted his tracks doubling back toward the woods. One of the dog's heel pads had a bloody gash in it and had inscribed the ice. Cider spat and shouldered the pick and shovel and made his way to the orchard clearing. Patches of icy snow still hung on in the shadows, and half eaten apples lay where the deer had cleaved them from the once frozen ground. The clearing itself was bone dry for the first foot and down from that the soil was moist and he got through it without trouble.

An hour later he had about finished the hole and he was down in it digging in rote mindlessness when Rance appeared on the edge of the grave, clutching a bottle of hell's blood in nothing but his underwear. "That's a damn good hole, boy," he said. "Your ma would be proud." He could barely stand, and when he rocked his arms went out and his toes gripped the soft dirt until he could recover his balance. He looked around.

"Where's that sumbitchin brother a yours?" Then he took a drink, retched, and wiped his mouth.

"You look like hell," Cider said.

Rance burped weakly and dropped the empty bottle into the hole with Cider and turned toward the house.

"Where you going?"

"Back to bed, boy. Where do you think?"

"What about Mama?"

"Barn's plenty cool," Rance said. "She'll keep."

———— ∞ ————

The next morning, Cider rose early, dressed, strapped on the Colt, and walked to Neff's to tell him of the news of his brother's and mother's deaths. Neff would not be surprised by Sara's passing: She had been struggling with pneumonia for months. But Gil's death was another matter. No one save Jasper could have seen it coming. Neff was inside making coffee when Cider knocked on his door.

"Morning to you," Neff said. He took one look at Cider's face and he knew that things were wrong. "Come on in and sit down."

"Thank you." Cider took a seat at the table and Neff sat across from him.

"You had your breakfast?" he asked.

"No sir."

"You want some eggs? I've got some nice bacon in the ice box."

"No sir, thank you."

"You're sure? Ain't no trouble." Neff's kindness poked holes in the dam and suddenly the whole thing gave and Cider sobbed. Neff gave him time. He was too far away to touch Cider's arm, but he thought about it. When Cider calmed down, Neff assumed Sara had passed and he said he was sorry and that there were few harder things in life than losing a loved one, and it was especially hard when that someone was your mama.

"She was as fine a woman as I have ever known, and she and your pa were my friends," he said. "How's Gil?"

Cider wouldn't look at Neff until he had wiped his eyes and gotten control of his face. He shook his head and again he could feel the sadness rising from his stomach. He took a drink of Neff's coffee to keep it down.

"He's dead."

"My God," Neff said. And for the next while Cider told the story of the last few days, how Rance had driven off Gil for reasons known only to them; how Gil had then killed himself and Cider had buried him for fear the news of his death would destroy what little strength Sara still had; how his precaution was for nothing. When Cider told Neff about the apples and how he planned to dupe Rance, Neff nodded and smiled at his cleverness.

"Good thinking," he said.

"But my problem still ain't solved."

"Because of Rance?"

"Yes sir."

"Hmm," Neff said.

"I don't know how I'm going to get him out of the house. From the day he started to work for us, he's dug himself in like a tick."

"He always did have a thing for your ma; anyone with eyes could see that."

"I guess you saw that coming?"

"Yes I did, but she needed the help; can't blame her for surviving, can you?"

"No sir, I guess I can't."

"So what are you going to do?"

"Bury those apples," Cider said.

"Then what?"

"I guess we'll see."

"Alright," Neff said. "You let me know what I can do."

"The burial's this afternoon." Cider wore the hint of a grin.

"I'll be there."

"Thank you." Cider got up and put on his hat.

Scraggly thing, Neff thought.

Cider was about through the door when Neff called to him.

"Cider."

"Yes sir."

"What are fixing to do with that Colt?"

Cider looked at the gun and then at Neff.

"Whatever needs to be done, I reckon."

<hr />

Rance and the dogs were sitting on the porch when Cider walked into the yard. A breeze carried the sweet smell of manure piled over at the Allred place. A fresh bottle of hell's blood sat on the railing and Rance had a plate of food on his lap and the dogs were eating raw eggs off Sara's good china. At Cider's approach, Dime and Slowdee came down the porch and walked half way out to meet him. Cider put his hand on the Colt and the dogs saw his demeanor change and they slunk under the porch.

"Where'd you disappear to, boy? They's pigs to feed." Rance carelessly set his plate on the railing and it tipped off and shattered.

"Damn it, Rance."

"You should be thanking me, boy: That there is one less dish for you to wash and put away."

Cider shook his head and climbed the stairs.

"Hold up there, youngster." Rance took a big pull of whiskey.

"What do you want?"

"Dog shit on the porch there," Rance said, pointing to the end of the porch.

"So?"

"Someone's got to clean it up; ain't my dogs, ain't my house; ain't that what you and your crazy brother always reminding me of since the day I got here?"

"He isn't crazy." Cider picked up a couple of the plate shards and walked to the corner of the porch. A pile of excrement sat coiled there like a headless snake.

"As a shit house rat, he is," Rance said.

Cider could identify scats of all kinds from his hunting days and he knew that turd didn't come from a dog. It reeked of whiskey.

"You sure a dog made this?"

"Hell yes I'm sure." Rance took another big drink and smirked. "You think I'm lying?"

"I didn't say that."

Rance sat up and put the bottle on the railing.

"Well what then?"

"A dog didn't make this turd," Cider said, laying the shards on the railing.

"How's that?" Rance asked.

"Dogs don't drink whiskey."

At that Rance took the whiskey from the railing and drank.

"This one does," he said. Then he leaned back in the chair and closed his eyes. "Boy, there ain't a man been born as luckless as me. First time I set eyes on your ma I knew I was supposed to be with her. I ain't prayed a day in my life, but I tell you I thought I was blessed when Preston up and died and your ma put out the word she was looking for help around here. Course I'd be lying just as sure as I'm sitting here if I said I was happy about having you pecker heads around, but had you not been I'd have to say the world is a perfect place and I've known all along that it ain't. Your ma dying on me is proof of that." Rance opened his eyes, took another drink, and looked at Cider. "You understand what I'm saying, boy? Course you don't."

Cider moved for the stairs.

"Where you going now, boy? I'm talking to you," Rance slurred.

"I got things to do before the burial." Cider walked down the steps.

"I'm telling you to hold up."

"What do you want?"

Rance took and released a deep breath and Cider could smell the whiskey.

"You think because you're wearing that gun that makes you a man?"

"I never said anything about being a man."

"That's good, youngster; cause you got shadows in you is all, the kind your ma's dresses throw when they hanging out to dry, or the fleeing kind of shadow, the kind something makes when it's running for its life. But shadows ain't true darkness, boy, and you ain't got none of that in you." Rance leaned back again and closed his eyes. He licked his lower lip and Cider saw that his tongue was cracked and swollen like a piece of meat in a jar of water. "That's what man is. His life is rooted in darkness. If your pa was here, he'd tell you as much. You can be sure of that."

Red-winged blackbirds sang their liquid songs in the fields beyond the orchard as Neff came down the road on his horse. A black, wide-brimmed hat sat atop his head and for the fifth time in his life he was smartly dressed. The barn door was open and he rode straight in and put the horse in the stall next to Rance's mare. He looked in on her and she was fine. All the other horses were gone and in their places were memories. After Preston died, Sara sold them off to buy supplies. She had loved those horses, and except for that emptiness, that flutter of knowing something is gone for good, she had given them up without hesitation. That's what people did.

Neff spoke to his horse and told him the deal and he closed the stall door. He glanced into the next stall and saw a marmalade cat stretched out in the hay. Many an evening he had seen the big orange cat asleep on Sara's lap and he knew his name was Codger. Neff watched and from where he stood he could not tell if the cat were breathing. When he called to it the cat did not move and Neff looked out the barn door and decided that whatever was out there could wait. He opened the stall door and knelt in the hay. His horse watched him. "Hey old man," Neff said to the cat.

The cat's eyes were still moist, but they were far away. He was breathing, but just barely. The ants hadn't waited to claim him and already they were gathering around his mouth and crawling into his ears. "Get out a there, you little bastards." Neff knew he was no better than the ants. For what living thing doesn't fatten itself on life so that it might stretch its years and live out its days without need and want? And yet the cat reminded him of himself and of Sara and of finer days and in a moment of wishful thinking he decided to do what he could to protect it.

If ever the ants were to visit him in the vulnerability of death, he would be grateful if someone were to send the throng of crawling mouths on their way until he could make his exit. "You're about done here, eh bud?" Neff pinched off the ants that had concentrated around the cat's eyes and mouth. Then he ran his hand over the cat and felt the soft coldness of his bones and the faint tremors of flesh being devoured from within.

When Neff entered the orchard clearing, Rance was sitting under an apple tree with his hat pulled down over his face, snoring. The apple blossoms held tight in the trees and the crate lay by the open grave. Neff thought of all those apples rotting in the dark and then he thought of Sara and Gil doing the same in the field. He walked over to Rance and tapped his boot.

"Wake up, Rance."

Rance pushed up his hat and webs of blood lay in his eyes.

"Aren't you a sight," Neff said. "Where are the boys?"

Rance stood and when he spoke, Neff could smell his foulness. "Cider's up at the house and I got no idea where Gil's gone to. Ain't seen him for days."

"You run him off?"

Rance took a step toward Neff.

"Maybe."

The two stared at each other and they were still staring when Cider came out of the orchard carrying a sack.

"Hey Cide," Neff said without taking his eyes off Rance.

"Hey." Cider studied the men. They had been reduced to clenched jaws and fists. "One a ya want to help me with the ropes?"

"I'll help you," Neff said, and he stepped away from Rance and he and Cider got started with the ropes. They straddled the grave, and as they lowered the crate, Rance walked over and took up the bag Cider had brought.

"What do we have here?" he said, searching through the bag and then pulling out the larger of two boxes. Once the crate had touched bottom, Neff and Cider pulled up the ropes and laid the coils on the ground.

"Give it here," Cider said, reaching for the box. Rance held it over his head like a child playing keep away.

"Hold your horses there, youngster. Old Rance just wants to take a peek."

Cider stepped closer and being a good five inches taller than Rance, he went for the box and, missing it, snatched the bag from Rance's hand instead.

"Ain't none of your damn business what that is. It belonged to Mama and Pop and it's going in the hole."

"Now tell me, why would you want to bury a perfectly good box?" Rance asked, stepping away.

"Give the boy his property, Rance," Neff said, but Rance ignored him.

"Nice box like this could hold your arrow heads or your jack knives or your tobacco when you get older. Hell, it could even hold your money. No, folks don't bury a nice box like this," he said, putting his thumb under the clasp. "They bury what's inside it." Then he lifted the clasp and opened the box. A wind swept by them and they could hear it rattling the leaves as it rolled away through the orchard. Rance appeared beside himself; his lips were gathered into a suggestive pucker and his eyebrows dipped into a "v" as he beheld the figurines. For a moment it appeared as if he were going to cry. Cider looked at Neff and Neff looked back at him and his face was full of alarm. Rance then scooped the figurines from the box and let it fall to the ground. The wind came again and this time it stayed.

"Give 'em here! They're going in the ground, Rance!" he yelled over the wind.

Rance appeared bewildered as he held the figurines like a litter of maladies. He kicked the box into the hole and then he looked up, his eyes brimming with water.

"I'll look after these," he said.

Cider and Neff could see that he wasn't in his right mind and so they stood by as he shuffled off toward the house.

"What in the hell has gotten into him?" Neff asked.

Cider pulled his shovel from the mound.

"I don't know," he said. "Whatever it is, it ain't from around here."

———— ⌾ ————

A few days later, Cider left the house just as night was coming on and he walked the road to Neff's place. The dogs followed him at a distance, stopping along the way to sniff the spore of other animals that had passed by there hours, days, and weeks before. The dogs had a penchant for wandering where they shouldn't, and more than once Dwain Allred had threatened to shoot or poison them if they came onto his property.

Cider wouldn't wish death on anyone; it wasn't in him. But whatever connection he felt to those dogs had died with Gil. If tonight they got themselves shot because they were shitting in Allred's field or harassing his cattle, he'd know their time had come. It was that simple. His time would come, too, which was fine, he thought, so long as it wasn't tonight, while he was walking to the house of his last friend in the world.

Now that most of what he loved was gone, he wondered at the dissolution of matter and during the keenest of those moments he found himself gazing at the dark places in the mountains to the west and to the deep, sunless gulches that cleaved them, and by that means he knew his own impermanence and the thought was new and strange. His life opened like a vein, and if it were true that one place is as good as another, then by God he would go there and see.

Large ashen moths flew in and out of the lamplight that fell through Neff's open front door. Cider climbed the steps and rapped on the heavy porch beam.

"Uncle Neff?" he called.

"I'm up here."

Cider stepped off the porch and saw Neff up on the roof with the stars and a thumbnail moon behind him.

"Howdy," Cider said.

"Howdy. Come on up; ladder's around the back."

"I'd rather not."

"Alright," Neff said, "I'll be right down."

"Thank you." Cider could hear Neff climbing down the ladder and a few moments later he appeared. "Stars falling on your roof?" Cider asked.

"Not exactly; thought I had a raccoon in the chimney."

"Looking for a den, huh?"

"I reckon so."

"Well, can't blame em for that."

"No, I most certainly cannot," Neff said. "I got some fresh eggs from Pickard. Interested?"

"I wouldn't say 'no' to some nice eggs if you've got some handy."

"I've got plenty; come on inside."

Cider sat at the kitchen table and Neff pulled down a

pan and placed it on the stove. Then he took a small basket of brown eggs from the ice box and set it aside. When the pan was hot, he opened a can of bacon grease and spooned a dollop into the pan and it slid across the hot surface. Neff tilted the pan until it shined with the grease and then he cracked six eggs into it and turned to Cider.

"How are things over at the house?"

"Quiet."

"Not in a good way, I take it?" Neff spooned the grease over the top of the eggs until they turned white. Then he plated them and brought them to the table and sat down.

"You could say that."

"What about Rance? He giving you any trouble?"

"Nah, he's been holed up in his room; I hear him in there talking to himself."

"He been going to work?"

"As far as I know." Cider took out a heavy piece of paper and laid it on the table in front of Neff.

"What's this?" he asked.

"The deed to my land."

Neff unfolded it and looked at the dates and signatures. Then he laid it back on the table.

"What are you fixing to do with it?"

"Hang on to it, which is why I'm entrusting it to you if you will allow it." Cider took a bite of eggs and Neff watched him chew.

"To me?" he asked.

"Yes sir."

"Why?"

"Because I'm going to wander for awhile and so far as I know, you're the only person I got left."

"What about Rance?"

"What about him?"

"Are you going to leave him there?"

"I ain't got the strength to get him out."

"I hope he doesn't wreck the place."

"Hell, he can burn it to the ground for all I care; might not be a bad thing. Besides," Cider continued, "the land is what matters."

Neff nodded. "How did you get so smart?" he asked Cider.

"Good teachers, I guess."

"Well, I'm going to miss you. Any ideas about where you're going?"

"West, probably; I figured I'd try to track down Ben and Mary; see if they're still alive."

"I figure old Ben would be about 70 now and Mary a couple years younger," Neff said.

"That's still damn old."

"Yes it is."

"I hope I live that long." Cider slid back his chair and stood. "What are you going to do?" he asked.

"Just what I'm doing."

"Alright. Well, I best be going." Cider pushed in his chair.

"You leaving in the morning, then?"

"Yes sir."

"When you coming back?"

"I don't know; I promised Gil and Mama I'd give them a proper burial and I'm going to try to keep that promise if I can."

"My grandpa used to say 'there are promises and then there are promises to the dead and you better know the difference.'"

"What did he mean?"

"I wouldn't dare speculate." Neff smiled.

"I'll keep that in mind," Cider said.

Neff looked at the front window and saw the moths beating against the glass, their tiny eyes reflecting the light.

"You need a horse? You can take Tin; he's a good animal, and he's young like you. He'll last a while."

"I'll be alright," Cider said.

"Okay then, well, you take care."

"I will," Cider said.

A couple miles away, Dwain Allred was sitting at the kitchen table having some pie and coffee when his son Jack came in, laid his work gloves and fence tool on the chair, and told him that two of the cows — a calf and a cow — were unaccounted for. He had found the fence breach in the far field and as he was preparing to mend it, he heard noises in Preston and Sara's orchard. Allred put down his fork and drank the last of his coffee.

"The far field?" he asked.

"Yes sir." The boy then asked if he could show him where and Allred said he could so long as his other chores were done and he stayed close by. Allred knew every inch of the ranch as well as he knew his own body, probably better. At fifteen years old, Jack had seen how his father worked the land and how the land worked him. The two shaped and changed each other just as they had since Allred senior had ridden into the valley many years before.

Jack watched his father as he took down the shotgun from the rack and loaded it. Then the two of them walked across the yard, through the gate, and toward the field. "Watch yourself," Allred said, pointing to a fresh cow pie. When he and the boy reached the downed fence, Allred leaned the shotgun against the post and studied the scene: The limb of a tree had sheared off and snapped the top two wires. The boy had hung a coil of baling wire on the post.

"Hand me the fence tool."

The boy patted his back and jacket pockets.

"Dang it," he said. "I left it in the kitchen."

"Well," Allred said, looking at the orchard, "you best run up there and get it."

"Yes sir."

The boy turned and ran back toward the house, and just as Allred yelled to remind him to watch for the cow pies, the boy slipped in one and went down. He stood and looked back at Allred and Allred shook his head and looked back at the orchard. When he turned around, the boy was running again and his coat was smeared with the stuff. Allred shook his head again, this time at the sight of Jack running in his old boots that were three times too big for him. Then he heard the calf bawling in the orchard. The other cows had gathered in small bevies and watched dumbly as Allred grabbed the shotgun and stepped over the wire.

It was full dark in the orchard except for where the twilight fell like a fine, white dust. Allred wore a light shirt and he could feel his skin tighten and shiver against the cold. The calf bawled in pain and worry, and in Allred's thinking there was no worse sound except Jack's crying when he was an infant. Allred was blinded by the darkness, so he waited for it to take shape and then he went in. The calf was caught in some loose wire and it had wrapped it around a tree and could not move. "You got yourself tore up, didn't you, you poor son of a bitch." The other cow was standing nearby, watching, and it never ceased to amaze Allred how useless an animal could be to its own kind. He put down the shotgun and took the calf by the snout and clamped down on it. He listened for his boy and then he yelled, "Jack!"

"Yes sir!"

"Bring me that fence tool."

"Yes sir," Jack said, "I'm coming."

Allred pulled at the wire and tried to walk the calf back the way it had come, but the bovine had pulled the barbs deep into the tree and into its neck, and he saw the calf's eyes roll backward and turn white. "Son of a bitch is going into shock." Allred looked at Jack and saw that he was breaking. "Go on back to the fence and wait for me," he said, and when the boy could not move, Allred left the calf and turned his boy and shoved him forward. "Get out a here."

The boy gone, Allred bent to his work and try as he might, he could not fix things. The other cow had not moved, and in the watery blackness of its iris, Rance stood pale, naked, and unknown as Allred tore at the wire and cursed the day he was born. The calf's tongue lolled and dried in the wind. Across the orchard, birds spooked and fled their nests in a frenzy of wings. Allred listened: The birds and whatever was spooking them were getting closer. Allred grabbed his shotgun and listened some more. Then he looked into the darkness and screamed for his son to run.

<hr>

As the moon rose over Soapstone Mountain, Cider felt its thieved light on all sides the way a wolf feels its pack. He could see the house, the place of his birth, and beyond it the cold green fields stretching to the river. A few yards ahead, a cat walked into the road and froze. A plump mouse kicked and stilled in the cat's mouth. The cat then turned and slipped into the grass. Cider looked at the moon as if for some reprieve and he wondered about the silence there and how good it would feel to sleep.

First light would find him on the road west, but in his thoughts he was already gone and had been for some time. The severing had begun with the death of his father, and one by one his roots shrank from the fields, rivers, and near and far mountains. And what is this life, he wondered: surviving malignance by love and sheer will, only to let go of what we love by violent or slow gradation? And what of his neighbors and the abiding world beyond the valley, for whom the Earth is the garden of heaven and hell? Would this place not always seem strange? Cider walked on. A barn owl called from somewhere in the dark. Farther out he heard singing and then saw the blotted forms of people around a bonfire, their hymns rising away from the land with the smoke and the ash, and only Cider was there to hear them.

EPILOGUE

By midsummer the snows had all but quit the mountains and the river had shrunken like a healing knife wound. Where the water had been now were smooth, bone colored stones, and in a light made smoky with pollen and dusk, stone flies crawled from the river onto the stones and broke out of their bodies.

When the sun had fallen far enough to burn away the filtering clouds and their shadows, those bodies could be seen with excisions down their lengths, and by means of this internal doctoring the flies rose into the air and into the silent throats of sparrows. The lead-paned wings of a fly lying longwise in a sparrow's beak like some exquisite mutation. And those bodies lay black in the moonlight. Strange hieroglyphics on the floor of the world.

Now with day a stone's throw from darkness, droves of trout moved up river feeding on the electric-green larvae of molting flies, and their backs shined like slivers of swimming steel. The fish rolled and vanished in their still haunts as though the river had shifted shapes where their backs broke and welled the slow water. Where the water nearly slept, the trout seemed to levitate in those clear depths with one eye upriver and the other on the top water where the soon-to-die mayflies gathered. If there were nothing riding the river for the sake of sustenance or breeding or transport out of the world — as it was for a gypsy moth floating into a bigger darkness like a letter sent who knows where — the trout gazed into the airless world above as if into a world long dead to them.

In the stillness of the cottonwoods, the river hummed with mosquitoes upon which yellow jackets and damsel flies fed. Water from the spring lightly seeped beneath the nude roots of the trees, and there a red railed fox sprawled and her belly, round and stretched and wide with cubs, lay heavy in the hint of the mire created there. To her the imagoes would return for meals of blood and all about her lay windrows of their cast-off skins, and there could be no worse place because this was the place of their birth and as such they would be forever compelled to return to it.

The trees draped jagged shadows and on the shadow's edge lay a fallen bovine of indiscriminate form that daily sank deeper into the loam and its hide stretched over its bones like a piece of crude furniture. The herd save for a few calves would graze wide of it lest they be stricken also and lest they disallow their dead to rot in peace and have this harbinger removed from their sight. The calves were wont to near the rancid mound, and they stood in its diminishing company as though waiting for it to rise. By autumn they would join in the wasting and thus they were schooled by the dead.

ACKNOWLEDGEMENTS

I am indebted to several people for sharing their stories with me over the years. Special thanks to Hans and Terry Carstensen and the ghosts of Crooked Creek Ranch. I also need to thank my father, Max Werner, and Guy Miller for their help in enriching this book.

Thanks to Daniel Wallace and Mark Bailey for reading the book and offering their expert feedback. A special thanks to my editor, Kirsten Allen, for helping me to see more clearly. And thanks to David Pace for his guidance.

I would be remiss if I did not also acknowledge Cormac McCarthy and *Blood Meridian,* as well as Sam Shepherd and his play, *True West.*

The editors of *Matter Journal #13: Edward Abbey Edition* also deserve my gratitude for publishing the first part of this book under the title *The Potter's Field.*

And thanks to Ron Carlson who, some 15 years ago, encouraged me to finish what I started.

MAXIMILIAN WERNER

Maximilian Werner is the author of *Black River Dreams,* a collection of literary fly fishing essays that won the 2008 Utah Arts Council's Original Writing Competition for Nonfiction: Book. Mr. Werner's poems, fiction, creative nonfiction, and essays have appeared in several journals and magazines, including *Matter Journal: Edward Abbey Edition, Bright Lights Film Journal, The North American Review, ISLE, Weber Studies, Fly Rod and Reel,* and *Columbia.* He lives in Salt Lake City with his wife and two children and teaches writing at the University of Utah.

Follow his blog at http://maximilianwerner.wordpress.com.

PUBLISHER'S MESSAGE

The closing decades of the nineteenth century saw widespread desecration of the ruins of Southwest Indian civilizations. There were few trained archaeologists, no ethic of preservation, and no permissions or permits required on public lands which held the majority of sites. Local and travelling pot-hunters destroyed and damaged thousand year old settlements, kivas, and burial grounds collecting pottery, tools, and even corpses to satisfy the growing demand of private collectors and museum curators in America and Europe. This rush on the ruins went virtually unchecked until growing concerns about the vandalism resulted in An Act for the Preservation of American Antiquities, signed into law by President Theodore Roosevelt in 1906. The Antiquities Act established policy and protection for archeological sites on public land, required permits for authorized archeological investigations, and imposed penalties for "any person who shall appropriate, excavate, injure, or destroy any historic or prehistoric ruin or monument, or any object of antiquity situated on lands owned or controlled by the Government of the United States."

At the same time, sheep and cattle ranchers brought increasing numbers of livestock into the arid West to graze the seemingly unlimited supply of free forage on sparsely populated federal lands. The herds grew rapidly. In 1870, 4.1 million cattle and 4.8 million sheep roamed 17 western states, but by 1900, 19.6 million cattle and 25.1 million sheep struggled on depleted rangelands. Attempts by Congress to legislate use of western federal land failed until drought and the Depression in the 1930s impelled passage of the Taylor

Grazing Act of 1934, which established grazing allotments and required permits for grazing on public lands.

Today, even these protections fail to eliminate the plunder of Indian artifacts and the destructive impacts of grazing on the West's arid ecosystems. In 2009, 17 residents of Blanding, Utah, were arrested and charged with more than 100 felony counts of theft and trafficking in Indian artifacts. And throughout the West, the herds of sometimes 15 ranchers or more compete unmonitored for limited forage in single grazing allotments, decimating deserts, young forests, and riparian areas.

Torrey House Press
http://torreyhouse.com

ABOUT TORREY HOUSE PRESS

The economy is a wholly owned subsidiary of the environment, not the other way around.

– Senator Gaylord Nelson, founder of Earth Day

Headquartered in Torrey, Utah, Torrey House Press is an independent book publisher of literary fiction and creative nonfiction about the environment, people, cultures, and resource management issues of the Colorado Plateau and the American West. Our mission is to increase awareness of and appreciation for the land, particularly land in its natural state, through the power of pen and story.

2% to the West is a trademark of Torrey House Press designating that two percent of Torrey House Press sales be donated to a select group of not-for-profit environmental organizations in the West. Donations also fund a scholarship available to upcoming writers at colleges throughout the West.

Torrey House Press
http://torreyhouse.com